The author of the Flipping Numbers series

PRESENTS

A HUSTLER'S DREAM II

ERNEST MORRIS

Good2Go Publishing

A Hustler's Dream II
Written by Ernest Morris
Cover design: Davida Baldwin
Typesetter: Mychea
ISBN: 9781943686568

Copyright ©2016 Good2Go Publishing
Published 2016 by Good2Go Publishing
7311 W. Glass Lane • Laveen, AZ 85339
www.good2gopublishing.com
https://twitter.com/good2gobooks
G2G@good2gopublishing.com
www.facebook.com/good2gopublishing
www.instagram.com/good2gopublishing

ACKNOWLEDGMENTS

First and foremost, I have to give thanks to the Man above for continuing to keep me safe. Whether it was in these chaotic streets of Philly or behind those walls, you have always kept an angel in my presence.

I want to once again thank everyone at **Good2Go Publishing** for supporting and believing in me. I never could have done this without you. You have devoted a lot of time, trust, and money in me to keep writing novels that will keep the fans wanting more. I hope that it continues to pay off.

To all my fans and followers, thank you for staying true to me and keeping me leveled. You are what inspires me to do what I do, and I truly appreciate you. I want to give a shout-out to all my Passyunk family. They took the buildings, but left the name, memories, and love.

Last but not least, to all my family and friends, thank you for having my back. I love y'all, and once again, let's get this money.

A Hustler's Dream II

ERNEST MORRIS

CHAPTER 1

Worlds and Fredd had moved up in the game fast as hell. To stroke their egos, they copped whips. Worlds bought a 2017 Denali with televisions in the headrests, front visors, and even one in the steering wheel. He had Lambo doors on the front that lifted up, and rear doors that opened like those on a Maybach.

Fredd kept it simple with a 2017 Lexus GS. It had a system so loud that you could hear it a mile away. Literally! The platinum rims blinded people when the sun was out. The leather seats warmed up in the winter and cooled down in the summer. It was candy apple red with wooden interior.

Worlds's Denali was black on black. They both had 2 percent tint on their windows, making it impossible to see who was inside. The two vehicles came as a gift, courtesy of Evani, who liked the way they were moving his product. He had hooked Worlds and Fredd up with his cousin who owned a dealership, and he gave them a great deal on the vehicles.

They followed each other down the block, and all eyes were on their cars. They pulled up in front of Roxy's, stuntin' on all the watchful eyes. As they stepped out of the cars, all the ladies stared and tried to figure out who the two men were. They were hoping to be the chosen ones who would get to leave with them that night. Even the niggas had to admit that Fredd and Worlds looked and smelled like money. Worlds walked to the front of the line and discretely handed the bouncer one hundred dollars as he shook his hand. He let the two men in as the rest of the people in the line stood there ice-grilling them.

"Let these ten ladies come with us," Fredd stated, giving him two more C-notes. He smirked at the group of haters, giving them something else to hate on, before heading inside with his entourage of women right behind him.

Worlds stayed on the floor instead of going over to the VIP section. He needed to mingle with the ordinary people for awhile so he didn't forget where he came from. He grabbed two stacks in ones and then went over to the stage. The dancer was killing the pole. She rode it like she was riding a dick. Worlds started throwing the ones at her when she climbed to the top and then twerked as she slowly slid down it.

"Why you not in VIP with everybody else?" Deja asked, walking up beside him.

"I'm having more fun down here with my peoples than up there. Feel me?" he said, swinging his arm around.

"That's what's up!" she said, tossing ones at the dancer. "This shit is packed tonight!"

"Yeah, it's wet panties night. You should get up there and show these bitches up!" he yelled over the music.

Deja smiled at him, giving him a playful shove. As the dancer leaned down, Deja placed a bunch of ones in her G-string.

"I'd put these bitches to shame!" She smirked.

Worlds laughed as they both headed over to the table where Fredd was sitting.

"*Assalamu 'alaikum*," Amir said as Worlds greeted him with a half hug.

"Wa alaikum salaam wa rahmatu-lah wa barakatu," Worlds replied, sitting down. "I didn't know you were coming here tonight."

"I brought one of my homies out here. When I saw Fredd, I knew your ass was here!" he joked.

He looked over at Deja and said, "You looking sexy as hell, lil cousin!"

"A bitch like me is always fly. Just 'cause I like pussy, I still keep niggas' mouths drooling."

She gave him a hug, and everyone sat down in the booth to enjoy themselves. Strippers were dancing around them, and they were tipping all of them. The vibe was relaxing until a couple of girls walked up to Deja.

"Excuse me, but was you at Vanity Grand a couple of weeks ago?" a dark-skinned girl with a long weave asked.

"Yeah, why? What's up?"

"You got my man jumped, and now he has a broken jaw because of you. If I didn't have this dress on right now, I would beat that ass. I will be seeing you soon, bitch! Believe me!" she stated as she walked away.

The girl's two friends rolled their eyes and followed her.

Deja sat there with a smile on her face. She wanted to grab the bottle she had on the table and smash it into the girl's face and give her a broken jaw to match her dude's, but Worlds held her arm.

"This is not the right place, ma. Let's enjoy ourselves, and we'll catch her and that nigga later!"

"I'm cool! I have to use the bathroom real quick," she said, getting up and heading toward the ladies' room.

As she moved through the crowd, she could see the girl who had just approached her walk into the ladies' room ahead of her. She looked around to see where her friends were. She spotted them flirting with some niggas as they watched them shooting water guns onstage at the dancers. Deja suddenly felt a rush shoot through her body as she realized this was her opportunity to catch the girl slipping.

When Deja reached the bathroom door, she removed her gun from under her dress and stuck it in her purse. She then removed a pair of brass knuckles and slipped her fingers through the loops as she quietly pushed open the door. Three ladies were walking out, leaving just the two of them in the bathroom. The girl was in one of the stalls. Deja set her purse down on the sink counter and waited for her to come out.

The toilet flushed, and the moment the girl stepped out of the stall, Deja hit her dead in the throat, causing her to bend over in pain.

"What was that shit you were talking now?" Deja asked as the girl fell backward holding her throat. "You're not with your friends now, bitch! Talk that shit to me now!"

The girl was gasping for air, when Deja kicked her in the stomach, ramming her heel into her ribs. She pulled her over to one of the stalls and slammed her head into the toilet.

"I don't know who the fuck you thought I was, but you should have done your homework, muthafucka!" she said, pulling her head out of the toilet. "You lucky I'm in a good mood; otherwise, yo ass would be leaving here in a body bag."

Deja smashed her head on the toilet again, this time leaving the badly beaten woman there in a bloody mess and still gasping for air. Before walking away, Deja spit on her and then kicked her again in the ribs.

"Dumb-ass bitch!" Deja said, flushing the toilet.

She checked herself in the mirror and then walked back out to the party. When she sat down, Worlds stared at her momentarily before he puffed on the loud he was smoking.

"You good?" he asked.

Deja leaned over and whispered in his ear, "All this shit that just happened has a bitch horny!" Her pussy was soaking wet from the adrenaline rush she just had.

"What happened?" he asked, feeling his dick hardening inside his jeans.

"I just beat that bitch's ass in the bathroom, so I think we need to get the hell outta here."

A woman's scream caused everyone to look in the direction of the sound. The girl staggered out of the bathroom with blood all over her clothes. People started shouting and running toward the door, trying to get out of there before the authorities arrived. Bouncers rushed over to her to see what had happened.

"Come on! Let's bounce!" Worlds said as he got up.

"Where y'all going?" Air asked.

"Your cousin just put in some work. I'm going to take her home. Hit me up tomorrow if you want to do something. Fredd, I'm outta here! Make sure you handle that shit for me too."

"Cool! I'm about to grab a couple of these bitches to take home with me. I might as well enjoy this money you're leaving!" Fredd exclaimed, holding up the stacks of money.

Worlds and Deja headed out the back of the club toward his car. The cops were just pulling up as they turned out of the parking lot.

"Where did you park?" he asked.

"My friend Neek has my whip. Let's stop at her crib so I can get it."

Worlds stopped at the light just as a car pulled up beside them. Its passenger side window came down, and he could see the barrel of a pump aimed at him and Deja. He hit the

gas pedal just as the first shot went off.

Boom!

The car took off behind them, trying to catch up.

"Who the fuck is that?" Worlds yelled out.

Deja pulled out her 9 mm from her purse and started

busting back at the car chasing them.

Boc! Boc! Boc! Boc! Boc!

"Drive this muthafucka, nigga!"

She kept firing at the car until she saw it swerve out of

control and hit a parked car. Worlds sped off all the way to

Neek's house, where he parked his truck in the back of her

crib.

Deja had already called her and told her they were

coming, so the back door was already open. They went

inside and locked the door behind them.

"Who the fuck just tried to kill us?" Worlds asked.

"I don't know! But that shit really got my pussy wet! Leneek! Bring your ass down here!" Deja ordered.

"Listen to your freak ass!" Worlds said, shaking his head at her. "Niggas tried to get at us, and all you thinking about is busting a nut?"

Deja gave him the middle finger as Leneek came downstairs wearing a pair of boy shorts and a wifebeater. She walked over and sat down on Deja's lap, giving her a kiss. Deja played with her nipples, making Neek let out a soft moan.

"You know what I need right now, so handle your business," she said, opening up her legs for both Worlds and Neek to see.

Neek got on her knees between Deja's legs and pulled off her thong. She could see Deja's juices already leaking from her vagina. Neek started slurping it up as she then stuck her tongue out and began playing with her clit. Deja leaned her head back and closed her eyes.

"Damn! Y'all seriously going to do this shit right now in front of me?" Worlds asked, watching them put on a show.

He couldn't take his eyes off of Leneek's ass that was poking out of her boy shorts.

When they didn't respond, he got up and walked behind Leneek. He squeezed her ass, feeling its softness. Worlds then pulled down her shorts and stuck two fingers into her pussy.

"Mmmm!" Neek moaned.

"That's right, nigga! Get your shit off! That's my bitch, so you can get it in with us," Deja replied.

He strapped on a condom and entered Neek from behind. She started throwing her ass back onto Worlds as he gripped her waist to keep his balance. Deja felt herself about to cum

and started moving her hips in circles on Neek's tongue.

"Oh, ma! Suck this shit!" Deja screamed as she squirted

all into Neek's mouth. Neek continued sucking on Deja's clit

until she busted another nut.

The two girls switched positions, and so did Worlds. He

lay down, and Deja straddled his dick. Neek knelt on the

couch with her ass up in the air in Deja's face. Deja started

fingering Neek's ass and pussy simultaneously, which drove

Neek crazy. She started biting down on the pillow. Deja then

started moving her tongue in and out of Neek's asshole like

a snake. Worlds kept lifting Deja up and down on his shaft.

He felt himself about to cum and slowed down because he

didn't want to cum too fast.

Deja felt his dick swelling up, so she grabbed it with her

pussy muscles and started working her hips. Worlds couldn't

take it any longer and pulled out just in time to explode all over her back. Neek came a couple minutes later into Deja's mouth. The three of them went upstairs to Neek's room to finish what they had started.

CHAPTER 2

"How many you need?" Rod asked the fiend as she walked over to the porch. Zy and Torey were sitting in the car talking to him.

She turned around to see who said it was. Her eyes then got big, and a smile came across her face. She strutted over to where Rod was sitting. "I was looking for you, Rod. Can I get a bundle until I get paid on Friday?"

"Fuck no! You can't get nothing from me until you give me the money you already owe me!" Rod blurted out.

"Come on, Rod! You know you're going to get your money. You can take me to the ATM. Please! I'm feeling bad right now," she begged while licking her lips.

Rod looked at the woman standing before him, with anger on his face. Even though she was on dope, she kept herself clean and put together. She had on a pair of black tights and a long shirt that came down just over her ass. Her hair was in a wrap, and she had on a pair of Jordans that Rod had bought her for her birthday.

"I said no! Now take your ass home and get away from this block. No money, no dope!" he said, waving her away.

"Who the hell are you talking to like that? I brought you into this world, and I'll take you out!"

Both Torey and Zy looked at each other and then back at Rod and the woman. Rod was talking to his mother like she was a piece of shit. Torey stepped out of the car just as Rod smacked her.

"Yo! Why are you putting your hands on your mom? I don't give a fuck what she does out here, but you better not ever let me see you do that again!" Torey said, helping her off the ground.

"That's crazy, bro!" Zy shouted as he hopped out of the car. "That's your mom, nigga! Show her some respect!"

"You okay, miss?" Torey asked.

"Yes, I'm not like this all the time. I know how to control my addiction, but I just needed a lil something to get me through the day."

"Where do you live at?"

"I live on Lindenwood Street. Why are you asking me that?" she said, looking at Torey.

"Come on! I'll drop you off and give you something to hold you over, but I want my money on Friday."

"Thank you so much, and I get my check after twelve o'clock, so you can pick it up whenever."

"Yo! I'ma drop his mom off real quick and grab something to eat from Popeye's. You rolling?"

"Nah! I'm going to count this money 'til you get back," Zy stated, already knowing what his friend was about to do.

Torey pulled off with Rod's mom in the passenger seat. He kept peeking over between her legs, looking at her pussy lips poking through her tights. She caught his glances and smiled to herself. She opened and shut her legs a couple of times before Torey stopped in front of her door. He then pulled out two bundles and passed them to her.

"Let me thank you for this," she said, placing her hand on his lap. "I can tell that you was thinking the same thing."

She began rubbing on the crotch of his pants, bringing his man to attention. She unzipped them, pulled out his dick, and then inserted it into her mouth. Her warm lips made Torey close his eyes and lean his head back.

"Damn, girl! Your head game is on point!" he stated, holding the back of her head.

He stuck his hand inside the back of her tights and made his way from her ass to her pussy. She was already wet. He then stuck his finger into her hole and started fingering her pussy. Seconds later, Torey busted his load into her mouth.

"Why don't you come inside for a few minutes? I can make you feel so much better," she said, sucking her juices off of his fingers.

"I already got what I wanted right now. I'll get at you some other time. I have to get back to my money right now," he replied, fixing his pants.

She stepped out of the car, closing the door behind her as Torey sped off.

He headed back over to Divinity Street to pick his man back up. He laughed at the fact that he just received a blow job from one of his worker's moms. However, his smile quickly faded when he thought about the fact that she was strung out on dope and he hadn't used a condom.

He pulled up to the crib and parked. When he got out of the car, Zy and Rod were walking out. Zy had a book bag of money in his hand.

"You ready, nigga?" Zy asked.

"Yeah! Let's slide over to South Philly and check on the other spot real quick before we shoot out to Delaware," Torey suggested, getting back into the car.

"Soon as I get another bag for y'all, I'll hit your jack, big homie," Rod stated.

"Alright, cannon!" Zy replied.

They pulled out of the parking spot just as Zy noticed a cop car coming up the wrong way. Torey also noticed it, and he was about to back out the other way, but an unmarked car was heading up the block. Something was about to go down, and they were right in the middle of it.

"Yo! Put the straps up. We don't want to get caught with the money and guns," Torey said, removing his weapon from his waist.

"Fuck that, nigga! We got work in here too, remember?" Zy blurted out. "Damn! We can't even run!"

"Let's just see what these pigs want with us. If they get out of line, we riding the fuck out. Tuck the straps under the seat for now. Just leave them close enough to reach for if we need to," Torey said.

Two detectives exited their cars and walked up to Torey and Zy. Torey rolled down the driver's window as they approached. "What can we do for you officers?" he asked.

"First off, you can shut off the engine and step out of the car," Detective Campbell said, pointing his gun at them.

Detective Henson and six other officers had their guns aimed at them as well.

For the first time, Zy and Torey noticed that there were more than just two police cars.

"What did we do?" Zy asked, stepping out of the car with his hands up. It would have been a death wish if he and Torey had tried shooting it out with them.

Even though they had guns, drugs, and money in the car, they knew they would be able to make bail. It was only twenty bundles, which they had in the stash box. But it was the money and guns that would be found.

The guns were registered to Torey's brother, who never had been arrested before, and the car was in his name as well, so they could say they didn't know the guns were there. Torey had already texted his brother with a code word to let him know.

After frisking the two men and cuffing them, Henson read them their Miranda rights.

Campbell had a big smile on his face, and Zy and Torey were wondering why he was looking at them like that.

"What's so funny, pig, and why we being detained?" Zy inquired.

"Let's just say you two have been some bad young men. Do you know a young lady named Nydiyah?" Campbell asked. "Before you answer that question, remember that what you say can be held against you in a court of law."

"Fuck you! And we don't know that bitch!" Zy said angrily.

"Well, it seems that she knows you, and she had some very interesting things to say about the night her friend and her brother were killed. Guess who was holding the smoking gun? Bingo!" Henson said with a grin, pointing a finger at the both of them.

Both Torey and Zy wanted to kick themselves for leaving the bitch alive. They knew the code of the streets was never to leave a witness who could point you out. Now they were most likely looking at murder charges. One positive was that the two detectives were so happy they had caught them that they didn't check the car, so they didn't find the guns and money. Zy and Torey hoped like hell they could get out of this.

* * *

Worlds was awakened by the sound of his phone ringing. He sat up in bed and then looked at the screen. He didn't recognize the phone number, so he silenced the rings. He got up and headed toward the bathroom when it started ringing again. This time he decided to answer the call.

"Hello?" he said, irritated. "Who is this?"

"Worlds, last night some niggas came through the block on some gangsta shit and shot Rel and Ant," the young bull said.

"Where they at now?" Worlds asked while taking a piss.

"I don't know! They put them in the trunk of their car and peeled off. Nobody has seen them since."

"Did you call Fredd?"

"I tried his phone ten times and got no answer. That's why I called you. What do you want me to do?"

Worlds went back into the bedroom. He thought about the night he had just had with Deja and Leneek, and his dick started swelling up again. "Keep trying Fredd's number, and I'll also try. Did they take anything?" Worlds asked while putting on his clothes.

"Not that we know of," the young boy replied.

"I'm in Philly now. I'll be there in about an hour. Round up some niggas, and let them know to strap up and be ready to move as soon as I get there," Worlds said as he ended the phone call.

Deja heard the conversation and was already out of bed and getting dressed. She threw on some black tights, a wifebeater, black Timberlands, and a black hoodie. She loved to get it poppin', and the thought of getting ready to bust her gun had her pussy creaming up. She removed the two chrome 380s from the dresser drawer and then checked the clips to make sure they were fully loaded. She then threw

on the shoulder holster and placed the guns inside.

"I'm ready whenever you are," she told Worlds, grab-

bing her skully and bulletproof vest.

"Let's roll, then! Niggas just grabbed a couple of my

coworkers, and we need to find out what the fuck is going

on. Muthafuckas have to learn the hard way not to fuck with

me!" he replied, cocking his hammer and then tucking it in

his waistline.

They headed out the door, ready to lay down anybody

who had something to do with it.

CHAPTER 3

"Ugghh!" Nestor snapped, flipping over the table. Food, fruit, and drinks went flying everywhere.

It had been a few days since his club had been robbed, and no one had yet brought him any information about the culprits who did it. Frustration was building all over his face, and everyone around him was beginning to notice it. Nestor stared out the window of his plush office.

While everyone started picking up the things that fell on the floor, one of Nestor's street workers walked in and closed the door behind him. He had his phone to his ear, talking to someone on the other line. "Wait a sec. I want you to tell him everything you just told me," he said as he passed the phone over to Nestor.

Nestor put the phone to his ear to talk to the caller. After listening to what he had to say, his face turned beet red. You could see the steam coming from his ears. He passed the phone back to his worker and walked over to his desk. Once he sat down, he looked up.

"Send some men over there, and bring him to me alive! Everybody else around him, you know what to do!" Nestor stated, lighting up a cigar.

"Got it!" the man said as he exited the office.

He looked at the people sitting around waiting for his command. They were all killers anxiously ready to put in work for their boss.

"Load up! We got work to do!" Chino said as he walked over and opened up the artillery room.

Everyone grabbed assault rifles and headed toward the four vans parked outside. None of the men said a word the whole time. They sat quietly with venom in their eyes.

"Where are we going, boss?" the driver asked, pulling out into traffic as the three other vans followed.

"Head over to West Philly. We are about to pull a snatch and grab. These muthafuckas don't know who they are dealing with. It's time to show these putas that nobody takes anything from the cartel," Chino stated as he pulled on a pair of black gloves.

The caravan got off the exit on Girard Avenue and headed toward Fairmount Avenue. The hit squad started checking the magazines in their weapons and taking off the safeties as they approached their target. Chino spotted the person he was coming for getting into a car and then pulling off. "Follow that car right there!"

The car was heading toward Lancaster Avenue. Once they got to 45th and Lancaster, stopping at a red light, Chino and his team made their move. The first van swerved around the car and cut in front of it, blocking it from trying to pull off. The second van blocked it from behind while the other two vans pulled up on the side of it. Chino noticed that there was more than just the one person he was looking for inside, and he knew what was about to pop off.

The van doors opened up, and the assault team hopped out with their weapons aimed, and ready for war. The driver of the car stepped on the gas pedal, and the car lunged forward into the van. The car rammed into one of the men as all hell broke loose.

The occupants of the car were far outnumbered and outgunned. The assault team's guns lit up the sky like the Fourth of July. Chino's gun was spitting out bullets like everyone else's, and in the moment, he wasn't even thinking about what his boss had told him. Although they got off a couple of rounds at Chino and his crew, all the men in the car were annihilated.

The sounds of cop cars approaching caused them to cease fire on the car and turn their weapons on the police. As the fleet of police cars came into view, the killers let their weapons sing another song. Bullets riddled the cop cars and their occupants inside.

"Let's move!" Chino ordered as he jumped into the van.

They peeled out of there before more cops converged on them, leaving what would be known as one of the biggest massacres in the history of Philadelphia. Over ten officers were slaughtered, along with the four people in the car.

Chino rode in silence, as he had to figure out what he was going to tell his boss when they returned. Nothing went as expected, and the end result was that the person they went to snatch was now dead.

* * *

Worlds and Deja arrived at the trap house to find twenty men waiting for them, all dressed in black. They looked around the room searching for Fredd, but he still wasn't there. He hadn't answered his phone all day. Worlds walked over to where his young lieutenant was standing and shook his hand.

"You ready to put in some work, cannon?"

"I was born ready!" he replied, cocking his burner and then tucking it back in his waist.

"Okay, lil nigga! I hear you. Has anybody heard anything from Fredd? Something is definitely not right, and we need to find him," Worlds said. His phone began ringing, and he grabbed it from his pocket.

"We haven't seen Fredd since the club. He hasn't even been here to pick up no money or anything," the bull replied.

"Let me take this call, and I'll get back to you in a few minutes," Worlds said while walking away to answer the call.

Deja followed him into the kitchen.

"This is a free call from an inmate in the Philadelphia prison system," the operator announced.

Worlds waited for the operator to finish, and he then pressed 1 to accept the call.

"What's good with you, Zy?" he asked, placing the phone on speaker so Deja could hear.

"Yo! Me and Torey got pinched on a murder charge 'cause of some bitch. We at CFCF on State Road. I tried to hit Fredd up, but he's not answering. Can you get us a lawyer to get us up out of here?" Zy asked.

"Yeah! We've been trying his jack too, but with no response. I'm going to send someone over to munch with some cash to try and find out what's going on."

"Thanks, man! This shit has been fucked up ever since we hit that club and took that work. That nigga really been acting funny!" Zy said.

"Yo! Watch what you're saying on here, and what the fuck you mean? Whose spot did y'all hit?" Worlds asked, not taking heed of what he had just told his man not to do.

"These cartel niggas. Fredd asked us to help him out, and we would split the proceeds. I thought you knew about that shit!" Zy replied.

"I didn't know anything about that, but let me get off this phone, man. You never know who's listening to our calls. If you don't hear from the lawyer in two days, hit me back up."

"Alright! Be safe out there!"

Worlds ended the call and then looked over to Deja with a surprised look on his face. She must have been thinking the same thing, because her expression said it all.

"Do you think that's what this shit is all over? He's been out there robbing people and didn't even put us up on game?" she asked in disbelief.

"I don't know, but I'm not gonna let nothing come in between my money, and I'm definitely not going to let my man get murked by these clown-ass niggas! So if they want to go to war, then that's what we're gonna do!"

"That's all it is then. If you're riding, then so am I! What do you want to do about this?" Deja asked.

"It's time to make our presence known in these streets again. So let's start by laying down a couple of niggas. I know I'm gonna die soon being out here. When death do come for me, though, it's going to have to catch me 'cause I'm not sitting around waiting for it!" Worlds said, trying to drop some deep words on Deja.

"Let's get it poppin', then!"

"Let me call my man real quick 'cause we can use his help on this. He's one of the niggas I know is about that life, and he'll have my back," Worlds said, dialing Bubb's number.

After talking with Bubb, Worlds and Deja gathered up their crew, hopped in about eight different cars, and then headed out to handle business.

* * *

Chino and his crew rode around the city wreaking havoc on every spot they saw, hoping to draw out the man who was behind taking their work. Blood was being shed, and it didn't matter if it belonged to the cops or the thugs. Everybody was getting it.

They pulled up in front of another drug spot that his informant told him about, and they watched the traffic going in and out. The spot looked like it was making a lot of money with all the activity that was taking place.

"Let's move!" Chino announced, stepping out of the van.

His men scrambled out of the vehicles on his orders, and in one swift motion, they rushed the house and shot everyone moving except a man and his fourteen-year-old son who were now being held at gunpoint.

Chino walked into the house where they were, and looked over at the man, who was looking very nervous at the moment.

"I found these two counting money in the other room, so I figured they may know something about your shit!" Chino's right-hand man stated.

"*Cual de ustedes cabrones robaron mi mierda*? (Which one of you bastards stole my shit?)" Chino asked the man in Spanish, noticing that he was Puerto Rican.

"I don't know what you are talking about! I haven't taken anything from anyone, and I damn sure don't know who did!" he replied confidently.

"So, you do speak English, huh? Well maybe this will refresh your mind."

Chino pulled out his burner, raised his arm, and shot the man's son in the back of the head. The silencer that he had slipped on before entering the house had muffled the sound, but it did nothing to limit the damage. Blood and skull sprayed out of the boy's head, and he crashed to the floor on his face. Chino pumped two more shots into the boy as he then stepped over his body.

"Why you kill my son? He had nothing to do with any of this!" the man screamed out, looking at his son's lifeless body on the floor.

"Tell me what I need to know, and you won't have to join him!"

"Fuck you! I already died when you shot my son. I'm going to kill you, muthafucka! I swear to God!" he said, sticking up his middle finger in Chino's direction.

Chino walked over to the man and aimed his gun at his face. The man closed his eyes and started praying in silence.

"It's funny how niggas always call on God when they get into trouble. Well he can't help you now!" Chino said, putting four bullets into the man's body and one into his head.

"We have to go, Chino. The cops are probably on their way, and we don't need another shootout with them right now," his man said.

"Let's go!" Chino said as he motioned for everyone to leave.

They all rushed out the door and scattered into the vans, leaving another grisly crime scene.

Chino called his boss and told him about the failed abduction and everything else. His boss wasn't mad, but he had given Chino specific instructions to carry out, and he hadn't. The boss told them to come back and let the goons continue to handle business. When Chino hung up the phone, he picked up the radio and gave everyone their orders:

"*Matar a todos los que tenían algo que ver con ella, y los echan a los tiburones* (Kill all who had something to do with it, and throw them to the sharks)," he said angrily.

The other vans broke off and headed in another direction while Chino headed home. He had to go deal with his boss.

CHAPTER 4

Josh and Fredd exited the SUV and shook hands with the two men who were still inside. They had just returned from making a meth deal. The money that Fredd had just made was going in with the rest of the money he received from all the other heists. He was then going to break off with Josh after paying him a hefty amount for getting him the buyers.

"Nice doing business with you guys. I'll let you know when I get some more work," Fredd told them.

"Okay, man. You have my number, so just hit me up."

Fredd said he would call them, but he knew his business

was over with then because he had sold all of the meth. The

only way he would get more was if he really wanted to get

into that part of the game. He gave Josh his cut and then

hopped into his car to get back to Philly. He had been gone

for a few days and left his phone in the car.

As soon as he pulled it out from the center console, there

were over thirty texts and eighty phone calls. He read the

first text, which informed him that there was trouble. He

needed to get to the spot. He first dialed Worlds's phone.

"Where the fuck are you at, cannon?" Worlds screamed

as soon as the line connected.

"You should know what the fuck is going on! It's

because of you that we are at war with the fucking cartel!

You need to hurry up and get back here. You have some shit

to explain, bro, and you have to be straight up with me. We already lost a lot of men. Zy and Torey are locked up because of a witness. We have to take care of that and get those niggas out of there!"

"I'll be there in about thirty minutes. See you soon!" Fredd replied, ending the call.

Shit had just hit the fan, and now it was only going to get worse.

Fredd didn't know they were robbing the cartel. He thought about what the man said before he was killed, and now it made sense.

Fuck it, though! Those niggas can get it too! he thought as he hit the gas pedal to get back.

* * *

Worlds was at one of the stash spots watching his workers package up the dope to distribute to the other blocks that were still operational. Since the war had started, they had been losing a lot of blocks, but they still had the main ones, that his men guarded with their lives.

He and Fredd had a long conversation about his treacherous acts and how he was interfering with their money. Fredd explained to him that he was just trying to get at some sure fast money. Worlds didn't care about what he was doing in the streets; he just wanted him to let him know so he could at least be on point in case something happened. He had Fredd's back regardless of the situation.

"I'll be back in a few, bro. I have to go drop off this money to Manda for the kids. We have to get back on track and handle our business. I'm going to set up a meeting with the cartel to try and squash this shit. You're fucking crazy, dawg. Out of all the niggas you could have robbed, you hit them!" Worlds smirked as he left the building.

He knew it wasn't as simple as he thought it was going to be, but he had to try something. If it didn't work, then fuck it! They would be going up against a whole fucking organization and most likely didn't have a chance of coming out alive.

Worlds pulled up to Amanda's crib and knocked on the door. She came to the door thinking it was her sister. When she opened it, her smile turned into anger.

"Why haven't you come to see your kids, Donte?" she asked, calling him by his real name.

The only time she ever called him that was when she was mad.

"I told you there's a lot of shit going on right now, and I can't be around you and the kids without putting y'all in danger. Stay off my fucking back, okay!" he snapped, passing her an envelope full of cash.

"Take this shit! We don't need your money, Donte! They need their father!" she blurted out, throwing his money at him.

He left the money sitting on the floor and walked upstairs to see his kids. Amanda quickly picked up the money and stuck it in a drawer. She knew the type of life that Worlds was living when she first started dealing with him. She even thought about the day when she saved him from going to prison when he murdered someone right in front of her. She had driven the getaway car.

Amanda looked around at the house that he bought for her and the kids and realized that he really took care of them. Even though they weren't together anymore, he made sure she and the kids didn't want for anything.

Worlds came back downstairs a few minutes later and walked toward the door. Amanda was sitting on the couch with her legs tucked underneath her.

"Are you gonna come back to see the kids later?" she asked, looking at him.

She really was trying to get him to stay with her.

"I told you what the deal was, Manda. I'll come get my kids when this beef is over. I can't put them in harm's way. There are some very bad people trying to get at us right now. I can't take that chance!" he said as he walked out the door.

After what Amanda did with his cousin, he knew he would never take her seriously again. He figured that since he was already in Chester, he would try to make amends with Dominique. He stopped at a store and picked up a couple of things. When he got to Dom's house, her car was in the driveway. He got out and walked up to the door. He tried using his house key, but it didn't work. She had changed the

locks when he left the last time. Worlds knocked on the door,

hoping that he didn't wake up her daughter. Two minutes

later, Dom opened the door.

"What do you want, Donte?" she said, with her hands on

her hips.

Worlds smirked because she also called him Donte. It

seemed like everyone did when they were angry with him.

He stared at her for a moment, taking in what she was

wearing. Dom had on a pair of pajama shorts and a T-shirt

that had "Juicy" written across the chest.

"I got something for you," he stated, handing her a long

box wrapped with a bow. "There's a rose for every month

that you put up with my shit!"

Dom wanted to smile, but she wasn't going to let him off

the hook that easily. She dropped the roses on the ground

and then walked away from the door.

Worlds picked them up and stepped inside the house, closing the door behind him. Dom sat down at the kitchen table.

"Why are you here? You haven't been home in how long?" she asked, looking at him. "What? Your other bitch kicked you out, so now you want to come running back here?"

"I came to make up with you because I missed you too."

"You don't miss me, nigga. My daughter asks about you every day, and I tell her that you're out of town somewhere. You're making money now, so you don't need me anymore, huh? I rode your whole bit out with you, and look how you do me?" she replied, with tears coming out of her eyes.

Worlds didn't say anything. He knew he was wrong, and he wanted to make it up to her. He never meant to hurt her the way he did.

"Why don't you let me taste that pussy, or are you gonna be mad at me forever?" he said, trying to put his hand between her legs.

"You ain't tasting anything, and how you come in here like everything is cool?" Dom replied, pushing his hand away.

But his touch had sent tingles through her body. She had to get away from him before she gave in.

"Come here, baby!" he said, moving in so close that she could smell his breath.

He kissed her, and she kissed him back. When he saw that she wasn't resisting, he started sucking on her bottom lip. He lifted her up off the chair and walked into the living room. Worlds sat on the couch as Dom straddled him. He removed her shirt to expose her titties. He had to admit, her nipples were huge. He forgot what he was missing.

He sucked on them one at a time while pinching the other. Dom helped him remove his shirt and rubbed her hand over his six pack.

He smiled because he knew he had his girl back as he lifted her up off him.

He then took off her slippers and gently began to suck on her toes. Dom sat there enjoying what was happening. She reached into her shorts and started to play with her pussy. It was so wet that when she pulled her hand out, it looked like she stuck had it into a cup of water.

"Baby! I need you to eat my pussy."

Worlds removed her shorts and spread her legs. She closed her eyes anticipating his next move. He stuck a finger into her moistness and began fingering it while his tongue played with her clit. This drove her so crazy that she kept trying to get away from him. He had a firm grip on her legs, so she couldn't move. His tongue moved from her clit to her asshole and then back to her clit.

"Damn! You know how to work that tongue, nigga! I'm about to cum all over that shit!" she said.

He looked up with his eyes and started moving his tongue faster. He stuck another finger in and then another inside until he had three fingers fucking her pussy. That shit sent her over the edge, and she came in his mouth. Worlds drank all her juices without letting any spill out. He got up and looked at her lying there with her eyes closed. She was still shaking from the orgasm she just had. She opened her eyes after a minute and acted as if she had a sudden burst of energy.

"My turn!" she said, pulling his dick out of his pants.

She got on her knees and slowly licked the tip. Then she started blowing on it, driving him crazy this time. She took all ten inches into her mouth without even gagging once. Dom was showing him that she was also a beast at giving oral sex. Her head was moving up and down like a bobble head.

"I need to get up in that pussy before I blow my top!" Worlds moaned, pulling her body to the floor.

She bent over on the couch, spreading her wet pussy lips apart waiting for him to enter. At first, he took it easy on her, until she said, "Tear this pussy up, nigga!"

That's when he slammed into it and started blowing her back out. Dom bit down on her bottom lip while looking back at him beating it up. The look she gave him sent him over the edge. He felt himself ready to explode, and he turned her over onto her back. She opened her legs so wide

that he thought he could see through her pussy hole.

He went right back to work, pumping in and out of her

love tunnel. The only sound that could be heard was that of

his balls hitting her ass cheeks. She grabbed her tits and

started sucking on them while keeping an eye on his dick

appearing and disappearing. She came again just as he was

reaching his. He pulled out just in time to erupt all over her

stomach.

"That was good, baby! You put that work in!" Dom said,

rubbing his head.

"I'm sorry that I hurt you, ma. A nigga had some shit to

handle out in Philly, and it has me stressed out. You just

helped me relieve some of that stress!" he replied, sitting on

the floor. "I'm not gonna lie to you. I have to go back out

there because niggas trying me, but I had to make sure that you were good first. I can't have you in harm's way."

"When will you be back?" she asked, getting up and putting on her clothes in case her daughter got up and came downstairs.

"Just give me a couple of days, and I'll be back. You still have that burner I gave you, right?"

"Yeah! It's in my room."

"Put it in your purse and keep it with you at all times. If a nigga gets out of line, shoot first and ask questions last. Do you understand me?"

Dom shook her head and watched as Worlds fixed his clothes and tucked his gun into his pants. He gave Dom a kiss before leaving the house.

She walked out her front door as he was just about to get into his car.

"Wait!" she yelled out, walking up to him and passing him the spare key to her crib. "That's so you don't have to knock when you get home."

He smiled, gave her another kiss, and then hopped into his car and pulled off, heading to his next destination.

* * *

When he got to Bubb's crib, he and Sunny were sitting outside talking.

"What's up, nigga?" Sunny said, giving him a pound, followed by Bubb doing the same.

Sunny was Bubb's cousin from the other side of Chester. When Bubb called him and told him that shit was about to jump off, he came over ASAP. They walked inside the house and went downstairs to the basement.

"I hope y'all niggas ready to go zero to a hundred real quick," Bubb said.

Bubb walked over to the light switch on the wall and flicked it off and on a couple of times. A couple seconds later, they watched as the wall slid to the side. The two hydraulic arms slowly made a low whistling sound to reveal a large vault-like room. The room was attached to the next-door home's basement. Bubb had bought the neighboring house and fixed it up. There wasn't an entrance to the basement there. You could only enter it through the secret wall.

"This is some movie type shit right here!" Worlds said, eyes wide open.

Inside the vault was damn near every gun you could think of. Bubb had a bigger arsenal than Worlds. There were rocket launchers, .45s, and different types of assault rifles.

"Where did you get this shit from?" Worlds asked, picking up a pair of night-vision goggles.

"We hit a train a year ago, and it had all types of military equipment on it. We grabbed as much as we could before the cops came," he explained.

"I remember hearing about something like that on the news. Fuck it, though! If these niggas want a ride, then let's do it!" Sunny replied, strapping on a vest.

They geared up, and Bubb closed the vault back up before heading out. The three friends were about to go meet up with one of the top men in the cartel. Evani had set up the meeting on the strength of Worlds being one of his top buyers. He liked his business and hoped that it would continue to progress.

* * *

The meeting spot was at one of Miguel's restaurants. When Worlds, Bubb, and Sunny arrived, they were escorted to the back, where Miguel was sitting on the couch smoking a Cuban cigar. He motioned for them to sit, but Worlds declined, choosing to stand just in case shit went south.

"So what would you like to talk about? I only agreed to this meeting because of Evani. Are you the one who stole my product?"

"No!" Worlds replied, stepping forward with a duffel bag in his hand.

He dropped the bag at Miguel's feet. It landed with a hard thud on the floor. Worlds stepped back, leaving it sitting there, before he spoke.

"I don't know what happened with my man robbing your place, but I'm a man of honor," Worlds began. "I would never betray the people who vouched for me, nor would I dirty my own or any of their names. A man's word is worth more than any dollar sign. That right there is every dollar you lost because of my man. I hope that brings peace between us, but if not, it's your move."

Miguel had to respect his gangsta. He cleared his throat, and about six coldhearted assassins came out of the back, wearing all-black fatigues. They had frowns on their faces and were holding assault rifles. They posted up around the room, covered all sides, and stood prepared to let their weapons bark on Miguel's command.

Worlds and his two friends scanned the room. The odds were stacked against them, but that didn't mean shit. Worlds wasn't fazed by any of the niggas in the room. The eyes don't lie, and he knew they were cold killers by their eyes. He had seen those eyes before when his man came to talk to him. He was quite sure that's why everyone exited the room so quickly when he told them to get out. E.J. was a man who demanded respect, and now looking at Miguel and his goons, they demanded the same.

Worlds wasn't the type to back down either. If he or anybody on his team was going to die, you'd best believe they were taking a couple of them with them. They all reached for their weapons, simultaneously gripping the handles.

The sounds of the click-clacks around the room echoed in harmony as Miguel's team peeped the move and clapped one in their chambers. Miguel's hand went up.

"Everybody chill the fuck out!" he shouted. "There is no need for bloodshed. Whoever pulls that trigger, even if it's by accident, will also have a bullet in their head before the other person's body hits the ground. Now stand down!"

The men did as their boss instructed. Worlds and his two friends relaxed just a little bit but were ready to pop off at the first wrong movement. Miguel looked at Worlds and then poured himself a drink.

"I know how niggas move. They fear what they can't understand, and they hate what they can't control," Miguel retorted.

"What is that supposed to mean?" Worlds asked suspiciously, with his hand ready to pull out.

"Nothing! Nothing at all! Your friend disrespected me in the worst way. I need him to be held accountable for his actions."

"That's my man, so I'm riding with him no matter what. I'm trying to show you a peace offering, but if that's not good enough, then this meeting is over," Worlds said confidently.

"Thank you for the gift, gentlemen. My men will show you out," Miguel said, downing the drink.

Worlds didn't know what the dismissal meant, but he was going to prepare for whatever happened. They left the restaurant not as satisfied as he thought he would be. He then made a mental note to give Evani a call to find out if the war between them and the cartel was over or not. Deep down inside he knew his team was no match for them, but pride would not let him just fold. Their reach was longer than the mob's, and he knew that they or their families could be touched anywhere they went.

Worlds, Bubb, and Sunny got in the car and headed to West Philly. There were some niggas out there who were also trying to get at Fredd. A birdie told one of their workers that the niggas with whom Fredd did business were going to rob and kill him. Bubb and Sunny were ready to put in work tonight. They didn't want to go home without adding to the year's murder count.

"So, who is these other niggas that we have to go deal with?" Sunny asked.

"Some niggas down the bottom on Melon Street. Fredd was fucking with them and robbing niggas. Now they trying to set him up, so we going to see what's good," Worlds explained.

"Where that nigga at? He should be out here too, ready to handle his," Bubb stated.

"I just texted him and told him to meet us at 40th and Fairmount."

"Okay, cool!" Bubb said, sparking up some loud so they could get zooted on the way.

They rode in silence listening to Jay Z's Hard Knock Life, Volume 2. They each had a Dutch of loud blowing as Worlds cruised down I-76 toward the Girard Street exit.

"If I should die don't cry my niggas. Just ride my niggas bust bullets in the sky my niggas. And when I'm gone, don't mourn my niggas. Just keep playing these songs my niggas. Say word to Sean my niggas."

* * *

When they went through Melon Street, nobody was out there. They parked on the next block and waited for a couple of hours. Fredd came and waited with them. He acted like everything was cool, but Worlds felt like he was too calm for someone who had a price on his head. His friend was really acting differently since the beef was squashed with the cartel. Worlds just chalked it up to him being on his grid.

"Let's roll out. We'll catch these niggas another day," Worlds said as he pulled off.

They were salty that they didn't get a chance to body anyone that night.

When Felecia had called Terrance and told him not to come home because niggas were out there trying to get him, he called Chubb and let him know. When they tried to call Robert Sean, he didn't answer his phone.

Later that night, they found out that the reason they hadn't heard from him was because he was dead. Someone had shot his car up when he and a couple of niggas were on their way to make a drug run. Chubb thought he was trying to burn them and do shit on his own with their money.

Terrance took it hard because they were the closest of the three. The news said that it was some kind of drug hit by the way the car was shot up. Terrance and Chubb thought it was from the robbery they did at the club, but how did they link it back to them? They had to watch their backs because shit was about to hit the fan, especially after Terrance got that call from the girl on his block saying that some niggas were waiting for them. They didn't know who it was or why they were looking for them.

"I think it's time to get out of Philly, dawg! If niggas looking for us, it's only a matter of time before they find us 'cause I'm not running!" Chubb stated, sitting in his crib on Hoverford Avenue.

"I'm not running either! You were right about that nigga Fredd trying to get one over on us, too. We should have gotten his sneaky ass. I thought we were better than that!" Terrance replied.

"Money changes everybody! That nigga is eating now, and we still riding around in your sister's whip. After we body his ass and get that change he's sitting on, we out!"

"Word! I'm with that!" Terrance said as they then remembered what Robert Sean's mom said, that they couldn't even give him a proper funeral and would have to cremate the body.

Chubb didn't even respond. He was thinking about how bad he was going to do Fredd when he caught up with him. Finally, he would get to torture that nigga and then blow his brains out of his head.

"I'm about to go upstairs and handle some shit. Make yourself comfortable, nigga. There's a blanket over there in that bin. I'll see you in the morning." Chubb chortled on his way upstairs.

Terrance chilled and played Madden 17 all night while smoking loud. His gun rested right on his stomach for easy access, just in case someone found them. He wasn't going to get caught slipping.

CHAPTER 5

Riggs lay in bed next to his girl, thinking about the chain of events that had taken place since he had been home. His girl's best friend had been killed, he had been shot and robbed, and now he found out that his own man had been the one responsible for it. On top of all that, his cousin had told him about coming up on some meth and that he was trying to get rid of it. The problem with that was his supplier had told him that someone had hit one of his clubs and gotten away with some work and money.

Riggs replayed that phone call his head. He felt as though Miguel needed to know what was going on. He wasn't stupid in any way. Fredd was Worlds's friend, and he knew how Worlds moved. Plus he had that nigga Bubb on his team with a bunch of young killers. It was only him and Drew, so he figured he would let Miguel's cartel eliminate Worlds and his team, and then he would take over all their territory. Miguel was no dummy though; he knew there had to be an ulterior motive behind Riggs's sudden actions, but he didn't care as long as he got all of his shit back.

"I have some distasteful news that I think you would find interesting," Riggs said.

"What is it?" asked Miguel.

"I know who was behind your club getting robbed," Riggs told him, waiting for a response.

"I'm listening," Miguel replied, tensing up at the thought of someone disrespecting him.

"It was some dude named Fredd. He was with a few dudes from West Philly. One of the dudes is the one that tried to get with your niece. His name is Robert Sean, and he lives right off of 39th and Wallace."

"How do you know all this?" Miguel questioned him curiously.

If it was a setup, Miguel would kill Riggs and his family. In fact, just the thought of him snitching made Miguel want to cut out his tongue.

"My cousin told me that he was trying to move some meth for somebody. I remembered you saying that someone robbed one of your spots. I just put two and two together. How many people in Philly know how to make meth? Look, I'm just letting you know what I found out," Riggs said.

74

"Thank you for the information. Someone will be dropping off something for you in about two hours," Miguel said, ending the call.

"Riggs, what's wrong?" Alexia asked, turning over and rubbing his chest.

"Nothing! I was just thinking about something. Those niggas that tried to murk me will be getting theirs sooner or later. They robbed some very dangerous people who take shit like that very personal."

"What does it have to do with you, though?" she asked, looking at him suspiciously.

"That's who supplies me with my work and helps me put food on the table or money in your pocket." He smirked, squeezing her ass when she stood up to put on her panties.

"I don't know, baby. However you look at it, that's still snitching, and we don't do that. What? He offer you something in exchange for it?" she asked.

"No, and that's not fucking snitching! Don't ever play me like that again!" he replied aggressively.

"Don't get mad at me. Anyway, I'm going to my mother's house to take her out for her birthday. I'll be home later," Alexia stated, heading out of the door.

She loved Riggs, but she was from the streets too. She knew that he had snitched, regardless of what he called it. If muthafuckas in the hood got wind of it, they'd most likely say the same thing. She just shook her head as she cruised down the block bumping Drake.

* * *

Zy and Torey had just been formally charged with two counts of murder and were now sitting in CFCF awaiting arraignment. There was only one way they would be able to beat their case, and that was getting rid of the witness. No witness means no trial, and no trial means no life sentences.

Detectives Campbell and Henson were pleased that they finally got the people responsible for the double murder. They hoped Zy and Torey rotted in prison with the possibility of no parole.

"Are you sure you don't want to relocate at the state's expense?" Henson asked. "You will have a new place to live, and we'll give you a new identity."

"Why would I need all of that if they're in jail? I'm not scared of them anymore, plus my mom is sick, and I'm not leaving her here by herself. I'm good. Thank you for the offer, though," Nydiyah replied.

She got up from the desk and headed for the door, slinging her handbag over her shoulder.

Detective Henson followed her outside to talk to her some more. A car was parked in front of the station, waiting for her.

"If you need me for anything, just give me a call. I don't care if it's day or night," Henson told her, passing Nydiyah her card. "See you at trial."

Nydiyah took the card without saying anything. She just gave Henson a head nod and got into the waiting car.

As they drove off, she couldn't help but think about the long process that a drawn-out trial would take. She hoped they took a deal so she wouldn't have to testify.

"What happened?" her cousin asked, looking over at her as they waited for the light to change.

"Nothing! Somebody broke into my neighbor's house, and I had to give them a statement, since I called them," she lied.

"Oh, okay! Are we still going out tomorrow night? They are having a party for my homegirl. She's about to get married next month."

"Oh, of course. I'm game. What time are you coming to pick me up?"

"Girl! Just meet me at my crib around nine thirty. We'll pick up my friend and leave from there," the girl replied, pulling up in front of Nydiyah's mom's house.

"See you then!" Nydiyah said as she exited the car.

When the girl pulled off, she made a very important call. When the person on the other end answered, she spoke briefly.

"She's going with me tonight. We will be there to pick you up around nine forty-five. Grab some loud from your boy so we can get fucked up!"

"I got you, and I'll be sitting outside waiting for you when y'all get here," the caller said, and then hung up.

* * *

Fredd was in too deep with the shit he was doing. He knew if he didn't stop, money wouldn't be made because they would be too busy beefing with niggas. He had just gotten off the phone with Worlds and was leaving out the door so he could go check on the stash spot in North Philly. When he pulled off, so did another car. The driver stayed far enough behind so he could see where Fredd was going but also not be noticed.

As soon as they got on the expressway, the car sped up and tried to catch up with Fredd. As soon as the driver was right behind Fredd's car, he hit the sirens, signaling for him to pull over.

"What the fuck these pigs want with me? I ain't doing shit!" Fredd said as he slowed down and pulled over.

The officer got out of the car and walked over to the driver's window. He motioned for Fredd to roll down his window. The whole time he had his hand on the handle of his gun. Fredd did as he was asked, to see what the officer wanted.

"What did I do, Officer? Why did you pull me over? I'm late for an appointment."

"If you don't shut the fuck up, you'll be even later. Now, can I see your license, registration, and insurance card, please?"

Fredd reached into the glove compartment, being careful not to make any erratic movements to cause the trigger-happy pig to shoot him. He gave the officer all the paperwork and watched as he read it over.

"Can you turn off the engine and step out of the car, sir?" the officer asked.

"This is some bullshit right here! I haven't done anything wrong!" Fredd said, stepping out of his car.

"Put your hands on the hood of the car, please."

Fredd did as he was directed. The officer patted him down to make sure he didn't have any weapons on him. He then asked Fredd to step over to his unmarked car. He placed Fredd in the backseat while he went to search his car. After checking out the car, the officer returned and let Fredd out of his unmarked car.

"Sorry for the trouble, sir. You have a good day!" the officer said as he walked back to his car and pulled off.

Fredd got back into his car and picked up the white envelope that was now sitting on the passenger seat. He opened it and smiled as he read its contents. He had what he was waiting for to take care of business. Having cops on the payroll was really paying off for them.

He had told Worlds that he wouldn't do anything crazy again that would put them in a situation like they had been in, without putting him up on game. But this was different. This had to be taken care of, and soon. He made the call to his worker, sharing the information that he just received, and told him to handle it.

After checking on his spots, Fredd decided to stop over at one of his shorties' cribs. He pulled up in front of Dwunna's house and saw that her car was there. He got out and walked up to the door. He didn't have to knock, because he had a key that she had given him when they first met.

Fredd entered the house and walked into the kitchen. He smiled when he saw that she was wearing nothing but a thong and bra. Her shapely legs, juicy behind, and slim waist instantly sent sparks to his loins. The stilettos that graced her french-manicured toes caused him to smile even harder. He removed his gun from his waist and set it on the kitchen table. He walked up behind her and wrapped his arms around her, burying his head in the creases of her shoulder as he inhaled deeply, loving the scent coming from her body.

"I could have slumped you just now. You didn't even know I was here!" he whispered as he kissed her neck.

Dwunna's head fell to the side as she enjoyed the feel of his lips against her skin.

"Hmmmm! That feels good!" she moaned.

She turned toward him and kissed his lips deeply and sensuously.

"A nigga won't never catch me slipping. Take a look under the towel on the counter."

Dwunna slipped out of his embrace and walked over to grab something from the refrigerator. Fredd lifted up the towel and saw the Glock lying underneath it.

He chuckled and thought to himself, *This is one bad bitch!*

Dwunna took everything seriously since being shot in the head while sitting on her porch. She carried her strap everywhere she went. He found her incredibly sexy. The fact that she was a rider impressed him. She had the street instincts of a nigga, and he liked that.

"Have a seat if you want something to eat," she said.

"What you cook?" Fredd asked, taking a seat.

"Steak and potatoes."

"And for dessert?"

"Me!" she answered.

Dwunna straddled him in the chair. The only thing stopping her wet pussy from soaking the crotch of his pants was the tiny fabric from her thong.

"Or you can have your dessert now!" she seductively said.

Fredd sat her on the table after pushing everything out of the way. He removed his manhood, and in one movement he slid her thong to the side. Her wetness warmed him as he slipped inside her. With one arm wrapped around her waist and the other bracing the table, he controlled the pace. He was slow-stroking her as their bodies moved rhythmically.

"Yes, baby!" she moaned as he kissed her neck.

His dick penetrated the depth of her that she didn't know existed.

Fredd's sex game was official. Each stroke made her hornier and hornier, and with every dip of his hips, she matched his intensity. She ground upward and threw her pussy at him as their bodies became one.

Fredd knew she had the best pussy around. That's why he always kept her on speed dial. If he wasn't out there doing dirt all the time, he would have wifed her. Only a few people had the privilege of sampling it, because even though she was in the streets, she wasn't a whore.

She closed her eyes and enjoyed the ride as she felt her orgasm build. She came so hard that she lost her breath for a moment. The pulsating tool inside her, along with the look of fulfillment on Fredd's face, told her that he had gotten his too.

"Wow! I don't think I'm going to be able to eat now after that!" Fredd stated, fixing his clothes.

"Well come upstairs and let me give you the whole performance!" Dwunna said, heading toward the steps.

She made her ass cheeks twerk to get Fredd's attention. Fredd grabbed the bottle of Amsterdam off the table and followed her up the steps. He couldn't wait to get some more of that pussy. She had him sprung.

* * *

Nydiyah and her cousin pulled up on 32nd and Tasker to pick up her friend so they could head to the club. He was inside the Chinese store getting something to drink. When he came out, he got in the backseat.

"Here! Spark up!" he said, passing them both a game filled with loud. They sparked them up and took a couple of pulls.

"Damn! This shit is fire!" Nydiyah stated, taking another pull.

"I told you, my nigga only has that good shit!" Nydiyah's cousin replied. "You want some of this Henney?"

"I'm good," the bull said, leaning back in the seat.

He had the Dutch in one hand while he was texting with the other.

After they smoked the loud, Nydiyah was feeling it. She closed her eyes and bobbed her head to the music. Her cousin finished drinking the Henney, and they were ready to get their groove on.

The dude they were with was sitting right behind Nydiyah, who was sitting in the passenger seat. He smoothly removed his gun that was tucked in his waist and placed it on his lap. He would have only a split second to complete the task, so he had to make it count.

He held up the gun against the seat and then let off two quick shots.

Boc! Boc!

Nydiyah's body slumped over in the seat. Her cousin screamed and tried to jump out of the car. He aimed the gun at her and squeezed off a round into her back.

Boc!

Her body fell to the ground, and she started crawling and trying to get away. He leaped out of the car and ran over to where she was.

"Please don't kill me! I have a daughter. I promise I won't say anything," she pleaded.

"I know you won't," he said, letting off four more shots into her body. "Nothing personal; it's just business."

Next he went over to make sure Nydiyah was dead. He pumped two more rounds into her head. He was about to run, when two undercover cops jumped out of a car, with their guns in hand.

"Freeze! Police!" one of them shouted.

"Drop the gun now, and put your hands in the air!" the female officer ordered.

She noticed that he wasn't ready to comply, so she placed her finger on the trigger. It was too late. He already had the drop on her.

Boc! Boc! Boc! Boc! Boc! Boc!

Shots rang out, and Detective Henson hit the ground. She wasn't wearing a vest, so three of the bullets ripped right through her stomach and arm. She let out a loud yelp and put her hand over the hole where blood was gushing out.

Detective Campbell saw his partner go down, and the suspect started to run away. Campbell let off four shots in the suspect's direction, dropping him in the middle of the street. He then ran toward the man lying on the ground.

The suspect tried to turn over and point the gun at the approaching detective.

"Drop it!" Campbell yelled.

But he didn't, so Detective Campbell fired a kill shot to his head and kept on shooting until his clip was empty.

More cops were approaching the scene in a hurry. You could hear the sounds getting closer and closer. Campbell ran back over to where his partner was lying on the ground. He started applying pressure to the wound. Cops started jumping out of cars and rushing over to where they were.

"We have to get her to a hospital now! Help me get her into the car!" he shouted.

Two officers immediately helped him pick her up and get her into one of the cars. Detective Campbell hopped into the driver's seat and sped off to get his partner to University Hospital. Even though it wasn't a trauma unit anymore, they tried to do everything to save her life because she was a police officer. Detective Henson died forty-five minutes later from all the blood she lost and the bullet that kept

circulating through her body.

CHAPTER 6

"A deadly shooting in South Philadelphia has left four people dead, including a police officer. Witnesses say they heard shots around ten thirty last night, and when they peeped out of the window, they saw a man running from the scene and falling facedown. Then a plain-clothed officer ran up on him and shot him at least ten times. We'll have more on this shooting as details come in. I'm Sahara Green from KYW News. Back to you, Carla," the reporter said.

"What the fuck happened?" Zy said, rushing over toward the television on the block he was on.

"Some nigga was murked by the police last night. He shot an undercover cop in the process, though. That muthafucka went out like a G!" the young bull said as they continued to watch the breaking news.

"I hope Torey is over there watching this shit. We might be going home sooner than we thought," he stated.

"Why you say that?"

"Nothing! Those cops were on our case. I think they were dirty and tried to set us up," Zy replied.

He didn't want to tell him the real reason he would be getting out. You never know who the rats are in jail, until you feed them some cheese. That's when they come out from the cracks of the walls and show their true sides.

"Damn! They probably were dirty. Look at all the shit going on out in Ferguson. They just shot and burned an activist, and everyone thinks it was a hate crime. But I think the cops had something to do with it because they didn't like what he was out there fighting for," the dude said.

"You may have a point, but I'm not into that debating shit right now. I have to go holla at my man on the other block. I'll get at your later," Zy said, walking back to his cell to put on his blues.

He grabbed his blue shirt and was about to walk out the door, when two guys walked in. They both were carrying something in their hands. They pulled the door closed, making sure they didn't lock themselves in. Zy noticed that what they were carrying were homemade shanks.

"You robbed the wrong muthafucka, dawg!" one of them said as they were mean-mugging Zy.

Zy looked at both men and knew he was not match for both of them. He would be able to take the skinny one, but the other dude was huge. He couldn't even get to his banger that was tucked under the bed.

"I don't know what you talking about, but whatever you want to do, let's get it!" he replied, showing no signs of backing down.

The two dudes started toward Zy, and he popped off, attacking them first. He caught the little one with a hang maker, which only stunned him for a second. The big dude grabbed Zy by the throat and started poking him in the stomach with the shank he had in his hand. The other dude followed up after catching his composure. They continuously poked Zy over and over again. Blood was everywhere, but they didn't stop until someone knocked on the door, letting them know that a corrections officer was walking around.

The two men immediately rushed out of the cell and ran into their own, changing their clothes that had blood all over them. They took the bloody clothing and tried to flush it down the toilet. After they changed, they walked out on the tier and sat down like nothing had happened.

Corrections Officer Johnson was making her rounds that she usually did when she came on the block. When she reached the second tier and walked past Zy's cell, she stopped with a look of horror on her face.

"Oh my God!" she screamed. "Code red! Code red!" she radioed as she looked into the room.

She rushed inside and tried to see if Zy was still alive. Fellow officers started to flood the block.

"Everybody lock in! Now!" the lieutenant yelled out as other officers started banging doors.

The medical department rushed onto the block, with a stretcher to get the wounded man. It was already too late, though, because Zy died in the arms of Corrections Officer Johnson. They still tried shocking him and performing CPR while they wheeled him out on the gurney, to make it look good in the eyes of the other inmates. They already knew the deal when niggas got stabbed up.

Torey was on the next block when they saw all the corrections officers running over to the block. He and a couple of other niggas from around his way were trying to see what had happened, when the COs on the block made them lock in. He wanted to make sure his man was good, but they threatened to lock him up if he didn't lock in.

"I'm already locked up! What you gonna do? Put me in the hole?" he said sarcastically.

The corrections officer that worked the block knew Torey was on trial for two murder cases and didn't really give a fuck where he was housed, so he tried to calm down the situation.

"I will let you know if your friend is okay. Just go ahead and lock in," he said, hoping Torey would follow his order peacefully.

Torey went to his cell and just missed them rushing past with his friend's body.

Later on that day, they moved Torey from the prison because they thought he was next. He found out his friend was dead, and snapped, trying to fight the guards as they tried to cuff him. He ended up in the hole over at PICC.

* * *

It had been three days since the prison had gone on lockdown. An investigation on who murdered Zy was still underway, with no leads. The warden finally cleared the lockdown, and the inmates were able to come out and take showers or use the phone again.

"Yo! That situation is done, but we couldn't get at the other dude 'cause they moved him," B.L. said.

"Where they move him to?"

"Over to PICC."

"Okay! That money will be in your account in about an hour. Let Major know we got him, too," the person on the phone stated. "Oh, and don't say shit on this jack again. You niggas are stupid in there. They record everything just so they can use it against you. I'm glad you didn't say my name so we would be having problems," the guy said before he hung up.

B.L. went over to where Major was gambling, and whispered in his ear. Major nodded his head and then continued playing cards. After the game was over, he headed over to where B.L. was standing.

"Yo! We need to try and hurry up and get out of here before they find out it was us!" B.L. said.

"Yeah, I wish we could have gotten to that other nigga before they found him."

"We should have just hung that muthafucka. It would have been less gruesome, and the pigs wouldn't have found him so quickly."

"Maybe! But let's get your people on the horn, since they're closer to paying that bail. My people are all the way out in Allentown," Major said.

B.L.'s real name was Bobby Little, and he was from North Philly. He had a crib on 12th Street, until he got locked up on a gun charge. He couldn't pay his bail because his girl

ran off with another nigga, and they took all of it with them.

That's why when this opportunity presented itself, he took it

ASAP.

Major went by the name Miami or Kendell Foster, and

he was born and raised in New York, but he recently moved

to Philadelphia. He was on his way to pull a job with a couple

of friends in Philly, when they got pulled over. The cops ran

his name, and it came back with a warrant. It didn't help that

they were in a stolen car and all of them were strapped. Since

they were near City Line Avenue, the cops took them to

CFCF.

His boys received million-dollar bails because they had

bodies on them. Major's bail was $200,000, so when B.L.

told him that someone needed them to put some work in, he

agreed. They were cellmates, so that's why their bond was formed.

"You make the call, and I'm going to use the bathroom before they try to lock us back up," Major stated as he headed for his cell.

B.L. made the call to his people to let them know to post his and Major's bails. The dude that hired them was going to put them on. They hoped they would be out by tomorrow so this shit wouldn't hold them.

* * *

When Torey called Fredd and gave him the news about Zy, he just shook his head like it really didn't mean shit. It was Worlds who was pissed that one of his men got touched. He wanted to get at whoever did it, to let them know that when someone touched one of theirs, he'd touch ten of theirs.

Worlds sent word inside the jail for information on who had something to do with the hit on Zy. He was just waiting for them to get back to him. He even put a price on their heads.

Fredd was sitting outside of a familiar crib with one of his men. He had met him when he signed the papers that released him from probation.

"As soon as you walk in the door, look to the right, and you will see it. Just grab the whole thing and get out of there. Here!" he said, passing him $400. "That's half now, and I'll give you the rest when you come out with the safe."

The man nodded his head and got out of the car. He walked into the building and headed up the steps. When he found the apartment he was looking for, he pulled out a piece of metal wire and stuck it into the lock.

Alexia was just getting out of the shower, when she heard someone at the door. As she walked toward it, she noticed that whoever it was was trying to pick the lock. She tiptoed over to the door and looked through the peephole. A man with a hoodie over his head was on the other side.

Alexia ran to her bedroom and into the walk-in closet. She looked around until she found the box she was looking for. She quickly pulled out the .44 Bulldog that Riggs had kept in it, and checked to see if it was loaded. The gun that he had bought her was in her purse, which she had left in the car.

Thinking that the intruder was about to open the door, she aimed the gun and waited with her finger on the trigger. When the first lock clicked, it startled her, and she squeezed the trigger.

Boom!

The gun knocked her on her ass as the bullet went straight through the door.

"Aghhh!" the man screamed out in pain as the bullet hit him in his shoulder.

He ran down the steps trying to get away.

Fredd heard the shot and immediately pulled out his burner from under the driver's seat. He looked at the front door and waited to see what had happened. Seconds later, the dude came running out holding his arm. He jumped into the car, and Fredd pulled off.

"What happened up there?" he said.

"Somebody heard me and shot through the door. My fucking arm hurts, man. I need to get to a hospital."

Fredd was pissed that his plan hadn't worked. There was no way he was taking him to a hospital, though. He drove until he came upon a cemetery right off of Baltimore Avenue.

"Yo! Grab the first aid kit out of the trunk," he told the guy as he pulled over.

The guy got out of the car and walked in back toward the trunk. Fredd opened the door and held his gun down next to his thigh. He looked around to make sure no one was around, and then aimed the gun at the guy's head.

"Wait! What you doing, man?"

"No witnesses! Sorry, bro!" he said as he shot him in the head.

He died before he hit the ground.

Fredd jumped back into the car and peeled off. But he was pissed off because he didn't get what he wanted.

CHAPTER 7

Worlds was sitting in Max's on Germantown and Erie waiting for Fredd to arrive. Lately, it seemed like they were having a power struggle on who was in charge. He wanted to lay all the cards on the table once and for all. They were equal in his eyes, but he was a better businessman than Fredd. Fredd didn't know how to move large quantities of work. He was the type to probably blow it more than get rich. That's why Worlds took care of all the deals.

Worlds kept looking at his watch and wondering why Fredd hadn't yet arrived. He already had been there for over an hour. Time was everything, and right now, time was something that Worlds didn't have a lot of.

"Man! Fuck this shit! I'm outta here!" Worlds said, putting a fifty-dollar bill on the table and then getting up to leave.

As he walked out, Fredd pulled up at the corner and honked his horn.

Beep! Beep!

"Yo, bro! Sorry I'm late. I got caught up in traffic!"

"Man! You got me bloody as shit right now, dawg. You really on some sucka shit right now. What, you couldn't hit my phone and let me know this?" he said, standing next to Fredd's car.

"Get in. I have to tell you something, bro, seriously!" Fredd replied.

Worlds hopped in the passenger seat as Fredd pulled into the parking lot up the street from Max.

"So! What the fuck do you have to tell me, man? I'm trying to get money, and all this dumb shit you're into right now is stopping that shit!" Worlds said.

Fredd began telling him about the Riggs situation and what had happened with his man trying to grab the safe from his girl's crib. Fredd listened as Worlds told him how stupid that shit was and that he should have waited to do that. Now he had no choice but to kill Riggs and his people. Worlds thought long and hard and formulated a plan in his head.

"You go grab the money from the spots, and I'll take care of this Riggs situation. We have no more room for error, or our big homie is going to dead our supply, and I'm not going

out like that," Worlds told him, getting out the of the car.

"If you need me, just call!"

"I'm good. I can handle this shit by myself," Worlds

replied as he walked off. "Call Deja. She's going to ride with

you to take care of business."

Fredd was really getting frustrated with the fact that

Worlds always wanted Deja to handle shit. He thought long

and hard about just putting a bullet in her head to alleviate

the middle man altogether, but that would only stir up some

more shit. Besides, that was only a thought. He would never

do something like that.

"Well, since he wants to handle shit, I'll just let her take

care of that, and I'll go get me something to drink," he said

to himself.

He called Deja's phone and told her to go pick up the money from the spots and to call him after she was done.

After talking to her, he made another call before getting out of his car and going into the bar. He was going to wait for Deja to bring the money to him, and then he would hand it over to Worlds.

* * *

Fredd, Deja, and Worlds were standing outside of the Carmen Suites Apartment complex waiting for two people that they hired to handle some business. Nut opened the door and invited them inside. When they walked in, Dev was sitting at the table cleaning guns.

"I see you still on some mob shit!" Deja smiled.

"Couldn't have it any other way! You know that prison shit is not gonna change a nigga like me. The streets is my life, and I'd rather be carried out by six than to be judged by twelve," Dev stated, standing up and giving her a hug. "You still look good."

"I know!" she replied while spinning around. "Anyway, these are my peoples I was telling you about. Worlds and Fredd, this is Dev and Nut. These dudes will put in any kind of work you need."

"What's up, cannon?" Fredd said, shaking their hands. Worlds followed up with greetings as well.

"There's a couple niggas out there that I'm not feeling right now, and I would like you to eliminate them. If we do it ourselves, the law will be all over this. I'm not sure what they know, but for some reason, my name has been coming up within the federal building. Now I have to lay low from putting my murder game down," Worlds said.

"Do you think it has anything to do with the fact that your man has been out there sticking muthafuckas up?" Nut asked, looking at Fredd.

Both Fredd and Worlds were caught off guard with the comment. Dev knew where that statement was going to lead, and he had his hand on his strap.

"Don't look so surprised. We hear everything. Those cartel niggas was gonna cut your hands off and feed them to their dogs, but your man stood up for you. They respect him, but not you," Nut continued.

"We didn't come here for that! So can everyone put their testosterone to the side right now. We are all on the same team, and we both don't like this nigga Riggs. So let's get at him," Deja said.

"I'm with that! He killed my brother, and for that, I'll kill him and his family for free!" Dev said.

"Leave his family be! Just get that nigga, and if you working for me, then you will never be working for free. This is for you!" Worlds said, tossing both of them a thick envelope. "Plus, that building next door belongs to y'all. Just cop from me, and you can do as you please."

Dev and Nut looked at each other and nodded their heads in agreement. The deal was now set, and they would be up for the task. That gave Worlds and his crew the opportunity to really focus on their investments and deals. Worlds was looking into some buildings to buy and fix up. He wanted to put Chester back on the map and bring some money to his city. Worlds, Fredd, and Deja left the apartment feeling confident that Nut and Dev would handle their business.

"Deja, since they are your people, they're your responsibility. I know you wouldn't just recommend them if they weren't about their business, but keep an eye on them.

Fredd, did you contact your connect in the federal building yet to see what's up?" Worlds asked as they headed for their cars.

"Yep! She said that nothing is coming up on their alert system yet, but that doesn't mean they're not going to be gunning for us soon. She said we should just lay low for now because our names are ringing in these streets right now," Fredd replied.

"Okay! Let the workers keep doing them, and we'll just collect the money. Speaking of money, I have to go meet up with Evani and Carlos to give them the money for our next shipment."

"You sure that's a good idea? The alphabet boys also might be watching them," Deja questioned.

"Their operation is squeaky clean. We definitely don't have to worry about that. They have all the bigwigs on payroll. They are my trump card when your people can no longer come through," Worlds said, looking at Fredd. "I'm going to get up with you later on tonight. Stop by my crib when you finish up."

They all hopped in their cars and went their separate ways.

Worlds stopped at his money spot, grabbed the money out of the safe, and headed over to his meeting. He made sure he called them to let them know he was en route. They didn't like people to just pop up without warning, even if they already knew he was coming. Their security was so tight that the president's detail didn't have anything on them. As powerful as these men were, it was important to be that way.

After Worlds left, he was going to chill with his kids and then go home and get Dom to show her the gift he got her.

* * *

Major and B.L. walked out of CFCF with big-ass smiles on their faces. Because of their bails being paid, they were free men. They walked out of the building and headed for Cottman, thinking they needed to get as far away from that place as they could.

Suddenly, an all-black Dodge Charger pulled up beside them and rolled down the window. B.L. got nervous knowing that he wasn't strapped.

"Don't get nervous, bro! Which one of you is Major, and who is B.L.?" Riggs asked, leaning out the passenger side window.

"You must be the man that gave us our temporary freedom. I'm B.L., and this is Major."

"Get in. We need to talk. And from the looks of it, you could use some fresh clothes."

"As long as you're at it, could you throw a cold Bud Ice into the equation?"

Riggs laughed as the two men got in the backseat. Riggs passed them a cigarillo filled with loud. Major took it and sparked up. After taking a few drags of the weed, he passed it over to B.L., who took it like it was his last meal.

"Damn, nigga! Slow down! That shit ain't going anywhere!" Major said, shaking his head.

B.L. took a few more pulls and then slid it up to Riggs.

"So, tell me all about the shit that happened in that joint. Where did they send that other nigga? 'Cause they are some dead men. Every last one of them!" Riggs stated.

He listened to Major and B.L. give him the play-by-play of the chain of events that took place, and he smiled realizing that he had hired the right men.

Riggs didn't have the money or the resources Fredd had, but he was going to hit them where it counted. In their pockets! He would hit every spot that had something to do with them. He figured it would make Fredd show his face, so he could put a bullet in it.

CHAPTER 8

Alexia pulled into her sister's driveway and parked. She got out of the car and grabbed the two large pizzas on the passenger seat. She walked up to the door and rang the doorbell. She waited about a minute and then rang it again. Alexis was about to bang on the door, when she heard the locks turning.

"Damn, girl! I told you I was on my way. Why did it take you so long to—" She couldn't finish her sentence because she was staring down the barrel of the gun pointed at her.

"I'm glad you could make it the party. Come on in!" Dev smirked, motioning her to enter the house.

Alexia felt like shit as she walked into the house. When she walked into the living room, her sister Aubrey was sitting tied up in a chair, and Aubrey's son was next to her on the floor. Aubrey sat there shaking, and Alexia could see how scared she was.

"What do you want?" Alexia asked, trying to figure out what this was all about.

Neither Nut nor Dev said anything. Nut opened the black bag he had sitting on the floor and pulled out the duct tape. Dev yanked Alexia down onto the other chair while Nut taped her hands and feet. Nut reached back into the bag and pulled out a pair of pliers and started playing with them, scaring both women. Aubrey's son sat on the floor playing with his toy car, unaware of what was about to take place.

123

"This is going to be a very simple process. So I want you to pay very close attention, because your answers will be what decide your fate. Nod your head if you understand what I'm saying to you," Dev asked, waiting for an answer. Alexia nodded her head yes. "Tell me what I need to know, and I'll let you go. Where is your husband?"

Alexia shook her head because she couldn't answer with the tape over her mouth. Nut removed the tape so she could answer the question.

"Ouch!" she screamed.

"Where is he?"

"I don't know where he is. I haven't talked to him in a few days because we had an argument."

"See, I'm beginning to think that this is all a fucking game to you, huh?" Dev replied, nodding at Nut. "You want to see why we call him Nut? Watch closely, then, and maybe you'll have a change of heart."

Nut walked over to Aubrey, who was trying to break free. He removed the tape from her mouth and jammed the pliers inside and gripped a tooth. With one quick, precise twist of the wrist, he pulled out one of her teeth. Aubrey screamed out in so much pain. Alexia watched as he pulled out one after another. She then had to turn her head, since she was unable to take any more of the gruesome scene that was happening before her eyes.

Aubrey's son began crying for his mom when he heard her start screaming. Alexia's tears started falling after she saw all the blood on her sister's face.

"I'm going to ask you one more time. Where the fuck is that nigga at? I don't want to hear that you don't know!" Dev said, pulling Alexia's face up to look at him.

When Alexia looked into his eyes, she realized that it didn't matter what she said. He wasn't going to believe her anyway, so she spit in his face.

"I told you I don't know!" she said.

She never would snitch on her husband, even if he did that shit before.

"I see you need some more persuasion," Nut said as he walked into the kitchen and opened the oven door. He removed the racks and then turned it all the way up.

"So you want to do this the hard way, huh?" Dev said, watching to see what his man was about to do next.

After the oven heated up, Nut walked over to where the little boy was sitting and picked him up. He carried him over to the oven. Without even blinking, he opened the oven door, tossed him inside, and then slammed the door shut. Not only could they hear the boy crying from inside, but they could also hear and smell his skin baking.

Alexia lost everything she ate that morning; it all came up and landed on her clothes. Aubrey had passed out from the insurmountable pain, so she didn't know what was going on yet. Dev even had to turn his head for a minute. He couldn't believe what Nut had just done.

"Michael! Nooooo! Please don't do this! Help him, please!" Alexia pleaded with Dev.

Dev looked at her as if she was crazy. He came for information and wasn't leaving until he caused someone a lot of pain and suffering.

"You can save him if you just tell me where that nigga is. I'll spare your lives."

Alexia didn't say anything. If looks could kill, Dev and Nut would be rolling in their graves right then. Dev was tired of playing around with her. He picked up a chainsaw and pulled the cord to start it. The sound woke up Aubrey.

When she looked over at her sister, she saw her bawling in tears. She could smell a faint odor. When she looked toward the kitchen and saw her son cooking in the oven, she lost it. Before another scream came out of her mouth, Dev severed her head from her body. It rolled across the floor right next to Alexia.

Nut walked up on Alexia and shot her in the back of her head. She slumped over in her seat. He then shot her two more times to make sure she was dead.

Next, he picked up Aubrey's head and set it on the kitchen table. He ripped out a cord from a lamp and tied it around the head to the ceiling fan.

Dev really believed that Nut should be in some kind of mental institution.

They both walked out the door, leaving the boy's body still cooking in the oven. Whoever found their bodies was never going to forget it. Dev hoped it would be Riggs who came home and found them.

"Now let's call that nigga and let him know that wifey stood her ground all the way until the end," Nut said, pulling out Alexia's phone.

"You had that phone the whole time and didn't say anything?" Dev asked.

"I just wanted to have some fun, that's all!" Nut said with a smile on his face.

"I kind of figured that out, but you know we fucked up with this whole situation."

"Yeah! The family was supposed to be off limits, but what's done is done! We'll just tell him they got in the way," Nut replied.

Dev tried calling Riggs from Alexia's phone, but he didn't answer. So Dev programmed the number into his throw-away phone and then tossed Alexia's phone out the window. When he called from his phone, Riggs answered.

"Who this?" Riggs said.

"That's not important at this point. What is important is the fact that you have pissed some people off, and for that, you have to die. I'ma keep it real with you. Your wife, her sister, and her sister's son are dead. Now we can handle this like men, in the streets, or we can come find your bitch ass. I prefer we meet up somewhere and handle this," Dev said, not sugarcoating anything.

Riggs was still processing what the caller had said about his family. His face turned red. His wife was dead? Her sister and son were dead? This nigga just signed his own death certificate.

"Meet me on 61st and Passyunk by Jack's Auto Parts. I'll be there in thirty minutes, nigga," Riggs said, ending the call.

He dialed Major and B.L.'s phone and told them it was game time and to load up. He fought the tears that were threatening to release, and replaced his emotions with anger. He put on a vest and grabbed his Mac II with an extended clip and a Mossberg pump, with a box of shells. He then left the house.

Riggs wasn't dumb. He knew the caller was referring to Fredd, and he hoped he came along too. That way, he could kill two birds with one stone.

* * *

Dev and Nut got there a few minutes early not knowing what to expect, so they stayed low. They noticed two cars creeping up slowly without their lights on, and they knew it was them. Nut was the first person to start letting off shots.

Boca! Boca! Boca! Boca! Boca! Boca!

He let his Glock with the extended clip spit with precision.

Rat a Tat! Tat! Tat! Tat!

Dev let the AR loose.

The cars stopped, and four men jumped out, letting shots ring back. They were inside the Jerry Corner lot on Passyunk Avenue. That's why Riggs had picked that area, because they were going to catch them slipping and sitting in the parking spot.

Riggs and his crew tried to flank Dev and Nut so they would be surrounded, but they were already anticipating it. The assault weapons were lighting up the sky as each crew tried to body one another. Riggs tried to run behind a wall and caught a bullet in the arm. Drew, Major, and B.L. fired in that direction to give him cover. Police sirens were heard in the distance and were getting closer.

"Let's get the fuck outta here!" Dev screamed.

He shot Drew in the chest twice, dropping him immediately.

They ran for their car, shooting wildly in Riggs's direction but missing everything. As they got into the car, the back window exploded, causing shattered glass to fly everywhere. A piece hit Dev in this left eye. He grabbed at his eye as blood leaked out.

"Get us the fuck outta here, bro!" he said as Nut sped out of the parking lot and headed over the bridge.

Riggs jumped into the car with Major and B.L. and headed back to his crib. He wanted to see what had happened to his wife.

When they arrived, the place was empty, so they drove to Aubrey's house. When they walked in, it felt like all the blood in his body drained out. He stared at his wife's sister's severed head hanging from the fan. Her eyes were still open, with a look of shock on her face.

Major had a light smirk on his face as he watched the man who hired him cry like a bitch. It showed his weakness, and they were grimy enough to use it to their advantage.

"How the fuck we working for a soft-ass nigga like that?" he whispered to B.L.

"I was thinking the same shit!"

"When we get back to his crib, you know what it is then. Fuck him! Money over everything! I'd turn on my mom if the price was right!" Major said.

That statement made B.L. wonder how serious he was about it. Should he sleep with one eye open? he thought to himself. He dismissed the thought immediately when he saw the smile on Major's face. Riggs was taking the death of Alexia hard. The three shots she had taken, he would deliver ten times as many when he got those niggas. If it wasn't for the cops coming, he wouldn't have left until they were all dead. To make matters worse, Drew was also dead.

"When are we going to . . . what the fuck is that?" B.L. said, looking at the oven.

Riggs and Major both looked toward the oven. They didn't even have to open it up to see what it was. Lil Michael's body was charred black and was still crackling. B.L. rushed over to the sink and threw up. Major couldn't even figure out what that little kid went through in his time of death.

"Let's get the fuck out of this place before we get blamed for it!" Major stated as they headed out.

135

Riggs ran into Aubrey's bedroom and went into the closet. He opened the safe that they had moved from Alexia's crib, and took out everything, putting it into one of her big bags that was hanging up. He then went into her son's room and removed the lamp, slamming it on the floor and trying to rush. He took the packs of ecstasy out and also put them in the bag. After grabbing everything he had there, he ran out and got into the car. They pulled off and headed to Riggs's spot. Using Aubrey's phone Riggs made an anonymous call to the cops about the bodies before he left, and left it off the hook so they could trace the call. That was the least he could do.

They rode in silence as they headed for Riggs's crib. Major drove, and B.L. sat in the backseat. Major had been plotting the whole time they were driving. When they pulled up into Riggs's garage, Major snapped. He pulled out his gun. Riggs didn't even see it coming, because he was lost in his own thoughts.

Boom!

The shot entered the side of Riggs's head, and his body went limp instantly. Major knew he was dead from the first shot, but he hit him again for good measure.

"Come on! Let's get the shit and get the fuck back so we can relax, man. All this shit has got me tired as hell," B.L. said, digging into Riggs's pockets for his keys.

"You go ahead. I have to make it look good, and then I'll get the car," Major replied.

B.L. ran up in the crib to grab the rest of the work and money while Major staged the scene to look like a suicide, not evening realizing that he had shot him twice. As he walked to get the car that they had parked down the street, he made a phone call.

"It's done!" Major said, when the caller answered.

"Good. Your prioritizing this will be rewarded. Check your mailbox in the morning," the caller stated before ending the call.

Major got in the car and pulled up in front of the door to help B.L. with the work and money hidden all through the house. They took everything and then got out of there.

* * *

Miguel ended the call and sat back in his chair with a grin on his face. He looked over to one of his lieutenants and lit his Cuban cigar. "One puta down, and two more to go! By this time next month, everyone will bow down to the cartel," he said, hitting the table with his fist.

His men nodded in agreement as they lifted their glasses and toasted to victory.

CHAPTER 9

"Damn, baby. Don't stop!" Dom begged breathlessly, opening her legs wider to give Worlds more access to her love tunnel.

She hadn't been sure it was possible, but she was able to place her legs all the way back, touching her ears as he practically pushed his entire face inside her pussy lips. The way he was sucking on her clit almost made her cum instantly. His tongue game was on point, and Dom was speechless at the moment. There was nothing in the world that could keep her quiet the way Worlds could with his tongue licking, sucking, and flicking through the folds of her pussy.

"Mmmmm!" Worlds hummed into her dripping wet box, tasting the strawberry flower coming from it.

His head game caused so much pleasure that Dom almost felt dizzy. She closed her eyes tight as he started lightly kissing her up and down her swollen clit. Every time he pushed his face into it, it made a sucking noise when he pulled away. Dom couldn't take it anymore. She needed some good dick, and she wanted it now.

"Baby, please!" she mumbled, with her eyes still closed, holding his head. "I want to feel you inside me now!"

She felt Worlds pull back before sticking two fingers inside of her pussy. Then she felt his warm mouth over her right nipple, sucking on it while he squeezed the other with his free hand. She almost screamed out loud, but she didn't want to wake her daughter. Her body started jerking, and although she didn't want to, she was about to cum.

"Not yet!" he ordered. "You better not do it until I say so!"

He pulled his fingers out and removed his mouth from her breast. Dom opened her eyes and caught a glimpse of him right before his dick entered her pussy, pushing her walls open even wider than she was ready to go at that moment.

The first thing that came to her mind was to meet his every thrust, but she was no match for him. He was tearing that shit up, and she loved the way he put it down. He was definitely winning.

"Oh shit, baby! I can't take it anymore. Shit! Tear this up!" she moaned loudly.

Worlds's phone started blowing up. He and Dom both groaned at the sound. She stopped moving her body so he could get up.

"Fuck! I thought I had it on vibrate!" he said. "I'm not going to answer it yet. Whoever it is can wait."

Worlds began pounding away again at her pussy like he was in a rush to bust his nut. Dom wrapped her legs around his waist and gave it back. They were in sync with their movements. She smiled in pleasure at the fact that he was putting her needs over his business affairs. The phone started ringing again.

"Aggghhh!" Dom laughed. "Just go ahead and answer it, 'cause it's killing my vibe."

Worlds grabbed his phone and shook his head as soon as he saw the screen. He didn't need to talk to them right now. He knew they were about their business, so he could speak with them later about the issue. When it rang once more, he figured something was up, so he answered.

"What's up?" he said, walking out of the bedroom and out of earshot of Dom so she couldn't hear his conversation.

"We had a problem with your car," Dev said, speaking in code just in case their phones were tapped.

"Where you at now?"

"Down the street from your man Bubb's crib."

"Okay. Go there and wait for me. I'm on my way now. I'll call Bubb and tell him to let you in," Worlds replied, ending the call.

He wanted to know what had happened.

He went back into the room and got dressed. Dom could tell something was wrong from the look on his face. She didn't press the issue, though, because no matter what, she supported her man. After getting dressed, Worlds gave Dom a kiss and rushed out the door. When he got into his car, he checked his clip to make sure it was fully loaded. He just wanted to be prepared for whatever happened.

A few minutes later, he was parking outside of Bubb's house. As soon as he walked in, Bubb, Nut, and Dev were sitting there with blank expressions on their faces. There was a lot of tension in the room, so Bubb spoke first to try to ease it before Worlds got the news. "We have Chester on smash now, bro. Everyone is buying from us, and if they're not, I'm sure I don't have to finish that statement," he said, giving Worlds a smile.

"That's great and all, but I know you didn't call me all the way over here to tell me that, so what is it?" Worlds asked, looking at Dev and Nut.

"We had a problem with getting the whereabouts of that nigga Riggs, and we ended up killing his bitch!" Dev began.

"Shit happens. She became a casualty of war. Did you at least get that nigga?"

"Almost! But he got away before we could kill him. His men was with him, and we only bodied one of them. We are going back through his neighborhood tomorrow thought," Nut mentioned.

"No! Go past there tonight, and if you need more men, take some. I want him dead by tomorrow morning," Worlds said.

"There's more!" Dev started, not ready to tell him, but Worlds gave him a look to continue. "His bitch sister and son were also there, and you know the rules of the streets: no witnesses. They had to go because they seen our faces."

They all looked at Worlds, waiting for a reaction to the news that Dev had just dropped on him. Worlds didn't want any kids dying, but he also knew that if they had left them alive, there was a chance of them going away for the rest of their lives. No one could risk that.

"Fuck 'em! They shouldn't have been there. Call me when that nigga joins them. I'll have something nice ready for both of you," Worlds said, throwing in another incentive besides what he already had already given them.

"Will do!" Dev replied. "We have shit to do, so we're out of here. That nigga will be joining his bitch soon."

They left out the door to handle business. Nut and Dev didn't want to tell Worlds the torturous things they had done to the little boy. They didn't want him to think about his own kids being tortured like that. If he did find out, it wouldn't be from them, and they wanted to get Riggs in the worst way. Little did they know that Riggs was already dead by the hands of his own men, or who he thought were his men. They were hired by an organization higher than any of them could ever imagine.

The next day when Dev was watching television, a breaking news story came across the screen informing that Riggs was found shot to death inside of a car in front of his house. Dev called Nut and informed him of the news. They were mad that they hadn't gotten the chance to put the bullet in him, but they were happy it was done. Dev decided to make it seem like they were the ones that put the work in. He figured Worlds wouldn't care as long as it was done.

* * *

Walid was on a Greyhound on his way back to Philly. He was just released from prison after getting his sentence overturned. It came so unexpectedly that he didn't even get a chance to call anyone. They made him rush to pack up and get his discharge papers signed. The real reason was they didn't want a lawsuit for holding him too long. He was sitting in the back of the bus by himself. When he looked up, he noticed a beautiful woman sitting in front of him playing a game on her phone.

"Excuse me! Could I use your phone real quick to call somebody to meet me at the bus stop?" he asked, getting her attention.

"Sure," she replied, handing it to him.

Walid called his brother and told him he was on his way to Philly and to meet at 11th and Filbert. At first, his brother thought he was lying, but when he heard people talking in the background, he believed what his brother had said. When

he hung up, he passed the phone back to the woman. He also

noticed that she was listening to his conversation.

"Thank you. I'm just coming home from prison. I was

locked up for a crime I didn't commit. They finally figured

it out and released me," he explained.

"Damn! That's crazy! Were you down for awhile?" she

asked.

"Just a little while, but I'm good. Anyway, what is your

name, and where you from?"

"Megan, and I'm from Atlanta. I'm going to Philly to see

a couple of friends. I just came home too. I was locked up in

Cambridge Springs for three years."

"Oh shit! So you just come home and already got a

phone, huh?"

"Yeah!" she said sarcastically but playfully. "I came home yesterday, but my friend wanted me to come down there, so she wired me the money for a phone and bus ticket. I'm only staying for a week."

Walid moved up to where she was sitting, and sat next to her. He wanted to get to know her. Megan was about five four, and she had brown eyes, a little thickness, and nice titties. She was a white girl, and Walid wanted to see what she was about.

"So do you have a boyfriend?" he asked.

"No, I'm single. So what about you? Do you have a girl?"

"I did, but she thought I was never coming home and stepped off with the next nigga. I'm Muslim, so I need to find me a wife, but she has to be on her deen," he replied, looking at her with lust in his eyes.

They sat and talked the whole ride, until the bus made a pit stop so everyone could stretch their legs and get something to eat. Once they got their food, they got back on the bus. Walid kept looking at her ass in the sweatpants she was wearing. His dick got hard just from thinking about what he wanted to do to her. Since they both were fresh out, he tried to push up on her. To his surprise, she told him that she needed some dick bad.

Since nobody was sitting back there near them, Walid told her to turn sideways. He pulled her sweatpants down and fucked her right there with no condom. Neither of them took one second to think about the other having anything. When they finished, both of them fixed their clothes as if they hadn't done anything.

The two of them conversed for the remainder of the ride, talking about different topics. By the time they reached

Filbert Street, it seemed as if they had known each other for a long time. Megan gave him her phone number and told him to hit her up tomorrow so they could have a round two. He stepped out of the bus terminal, and Chubb and Terrance were standing next to a car waiting for him.

"Lil nigga, what's up?" Chubb said, walking toward his brother. They hadn't seen each other in a while, and he was glad that he didn't have to do the time.

"I'm good, bro! Glad to be home."

They gave each other dap followed by a hug. Chubb stepped back to take in his little brother.

"Somebody been working out in that joint?" Chubb said, noticing how big Walid had gotten.

"I had to get my weight up in there, just in case one of these niggas tried to get stupid out here," he replied.

Chubb thought about telling him about the beef they had just encountered. But he decided to wait until later. Right now, they were going to get fucked up.

"You don't have to worry about that. Niggas know what it is in these streets," Terrance said.

"Here, take this!" Chubb told Walid, passing him a burner. "Just so you're ready and don't have to get ready."

"Get in, y'all! Let's get the fuck out of here and go chill with some bitches," Terrance said.

They all hopped in the car and pulled out into traffic. Chubb sparked up the loud while Walid popped open the bottle of E&J. They headed to the After Hour on Dekalb Street, a club that Chubb had helped open down the bottom with his man Nitty.

The place was packed when they got there. Walid got fucked up with his brother all night. He was going to get in touch with his older brother the next day to get back on. He

just hoped that he wouldn't be on some bullshit, since they

weren't that close.

CHAPTER 10

"Are we still going out on Friday night to Vanity Grand?" Neek asked Deja as she lay on her chest.

Deja's hand was massaging her ass. "Didn't I say we was?" she replied.

They had just returned from the bar. Deja was torn up from all the liquor that she drank, and so was Neek. The liquor had both of them horny as ever. Neek started kissing Deja passionately, working her way down to her chest. Deja closed her eyes and enjoyed the feeling of Neek sucking on her nipples.

"Let me taste you!" Neek said while kissing her earlobes.

Neek started sucking on her neck. Deja felt the anticipation between her legs. She grew wet instantly and took a deep breath as she tried to control the wild sensations taking place within the folds of her pussy lips. Neek got down on her knees, keeping her eyes on Deja the entire time as she spread her legs apart. Deja sucked in a sharp breath when she felt Neek blowing on her pussy and then placing two fingers deep inside of her moistness.

"Mmmmmm!" Neek moaned as she sucked on her fingers that had just been inside of Deja. "I love it when you don't wear any panties."

She smiled at Deja before pushing her legs even farther apart, making the dress she was wearing slide up her hips and out of the way. Neek dove in without hesitation and without even thinking. Her tongue was making rings around Deja's clit. *She has the best head game*, Deja thought to herself.

Deja had her share of men in her life, but no one could satisfy her like Neek did. Actually, there was only one other person that could give Neek a run for her money, and that was Worlds.

Neek slid her hand up under Deja and grabbed onto her ass, pushing her forward so her pussy was at full display in front of her face. Neek moaned, sucked, and licked her pussy lips as if she was eating her last meal. That feeling in Deja's body was approaching for the third time in the last ten minutes, and she couldn't take any more. She kept trying to push Neek away, but she wouldn't stop.

Neek stuck her tongue deep inside Deja's hole, and Deja went crazy. Neek's hair fell down over her face, and Deja wrapped it around her hand and then pulled on it, making her tongue go deeper inside her now swollen walls. Deja arched her back trying to meet each movement. The orgasm came so fast that it took her breath away. Neek lifted up just enough to slip two fingers into her hole as she used her tongue to tickle her clit. That is when Deja really exploded. Her juices poured out all in Neek's mouth and over the sheets.

Deja lay there completely exhausted. She pulled Neek up and began kissing her. She then returned the favor by pushing Neek down and diving in headfirst. They went at it all night long, switching positions. Deja fell asleep lying butt naked in the center of the bed.

Neek got up and put on a robe. She walked out of the room and went downstairs. When she unlocked the door, two masked men rushed inside with guns in hand. They pushed Neek out of the way and went straight upstairs as if they knew who they were looking for.

They walked into the room and saw Deja's naked body sprawled out on the bed. Both of the men instantly bricked up at the sight before them. One of the masked men walked over and cocked his gun, aiming it at Deja's head. He fired a shot and smiled at the hole he made.

"I thought you weren't going to kill her!" Neek said, rushing into the room, but not seeing any blood.

"Shut up and get out of the way!" the man said, wrapping Deja's body up in a sheet. They lifted her up and carried her out of the house, placing her in the back of the SUV. "Are you coming or not?"

Neek ran back into the house and put on her clothes. She grabbed her cell phone and car keys. She then locked the door behind her and hopped in the backseat.

"When do I get my money?" she asked.

"Miss! You will get your money as soon as we get rid of your friend. You got some of it when we agreed to set this shit up, didn't you?" the driver asked.

Neek shook her head and looked out the window as they drove through the park. She was nervous about what she had done, and hoped that it didn't come back and bite her in the ass.

* * *

Chubb and Terrance were standing on Melon Street talking to Byron and Bricks. They were two young bulls that lived on the block. You could see in their eyes and tell that they were hungry to get in the game. Instead of diving in,

160

Chubb was trying to school them. He sparked up the pineapple games they had bought from the Popi Store at 37th and Fairmount. They passed them around as they watched Terrance serve the fiends that came on the block.

"Can I bring you back five dollars later for a bundle?" the girl said to Terrance, holding out the short money in her hand.

"You can come back when your money is straight. Don't nobody take shorts on this block," he replied.

"Please! I'll do anything. My body really needs this shit now," she said, with pleading eyes.

Terrance looked at the girl and couldn't believe she was strung out on dope. She was a beautiful, young Spanish girl. He had never seen her around there before. She had on a pair of tights, and he could see her pussy lips poking out in front.

He looked over at Chubb and told him he would be right back.

"Yo! Let me holla at you in the alley real quick," he said, walking toward the path between his crib. The girl followed him, already knowing what it was about. "Let me see what your head game is about."

"So you're going to give it to me for free if I do this?" she asked, licking her lips.

"If you got skills, I'll give you two," he stated, unzipping his pants and pulling out his erect penis.

The girl looked around to make sure nobody was looking, and then she got down on her knees and took his dick in her hands. She massaged his scrotum, tracing each ball with her fingertips. Terrance enjoyed the touch and sighed from the pleasure. She opened her mouth wide and bit down into his penis with immense force. She pressed down hard on his dick, grinding her teeth while shaking her head frantically from side to side like a predator devouring its prey. Terrance squealed like a slaughtered hog and fell to the ground in pain.

Chubb, Bricks, and Byron heard the scream and looked over toward the sound. They walked over to the alley to see what was going on. When Chubb looked down the alley, the girl was standing on top of Terrance looking down at him.

"What the fuck are you doing?" Chubb shouted as he walked up on them.

The girl turned around and pointed a gun at him. Bricks and Byron quickly backed out of the alley, leaving Chubb still standing there. She no longer looked like a smoker to them.

"Whoooaaa, ma! What is this all about?" Chubb said, holding his hands up.

"Fredd sends his regards!" the girl said, aiming at Terrance and pulling the trigger.

Boca! Boca!

Chubb tried to rush her, but she was quick on the draw. She turned and fired three shots at him. Chubb fell face first on the ground. Knowing that someone heard the shots, the girl ran through the alley to the other side and jumped into the car waiting for her. They sped off down Fairmount Street.

Bricks and Byron had grabbed the guns that Chubb stashed under the car tires, and they ran toward the screeching tires. They saw the car speeding down the streets and opened fire on it. People were sitting outside and began to take cover so they wouldn't get hit by a stray bullet. They missed their target but sent a warning to whomever it was not to come back. They ran back to Melon Street and hid the guns. They wanted to see what was going on with their old heads.

Cops were coming up the block, followed by fire and rescue. Bricks stood outside his aunt's door and watched the commotion going on. Terrance was dead, and they rushed Chubb to the hospital. Detectives flooded the block, messing up everybody from getting money. Everything was shut down.

Bricks had Chubb's trap phone and saw his brother's number on it. He called to inform him of what had just transpired and to tell him what hospital they took Chubb to. Besides the phone, Bricks knew where Chubb's work was at, so if somebody hit him up for something, he was going to help his big homie out and show him he was ready for the streets.

* * *

Walid got the news about Chubb and was there twenty minutes later to check on his brother. He was in surgery, so he waited for the doctor to bring him the news. He kept trying to reach his other brother, but he didn't contact him, so he used Facebook and Instagram to reach him.

Three hours later, Chubb was out of surgery. Walid was able to go to his room to visit. When he walked in, Chubb looked at him and gave his little brother a slight smile, but Walid could sense something wasn't right.

"What's up, bro? How are you doing?" Walid said, walking over and standing next to him.

Chubb lay in the hospital bed with a colonoscopy bag attached to his stomach. He stared at Walid for a second before responding.

"The bitch should have killed me. What the fuck am I supposed to do carrying around this fucking shit bag!"

"Who did this to you? When I finish with them, they will never forget the Morris family," Walid stated, with venom in his eyes.

"I don't know who that bitch was!" Chubb replied.

While they were sitting there talking, a detective walked into the room. He carried a small file in one hand and his wallet with his credentials in the other. Walid and Chubb knew who he was before he flashed his badge. They could smell a cop a mile away.

"Sorry to bug you, Kevin," Detective Campbell began, calling Chubb by his government name. "I have to ask you some questions about what happened on the 3800 block of Melon Street."

"We don't know anything, so you can turn around and walk the fuck back out the door," Walid barked at the cop.

"Listen, Sedric! I know all about the both of you. I know what type of shit the Morris-Johnson family is into, so miss me with that bullshit you talking. You already lost one brother to the streets. Do you want to lose another one?"

The detective was referring to their brother who everyone thought was dead but was living a whole new life in Florida. Only a few people knew he was alive and well. That's how he wanted it to be until he was able to once again walk the streets of Philly. He was actually going to change his facial identity as well.

Chubb just sat there listening to his brother and the cop argue back and forth. If he wasn't in so much pain, he would have been involved too. He listened intently to what the detective was saying, as thoughts flashed through his mind.

"We have nothing to say to you, so can you roll out and let my brother rest!" Walid barked, walking over to the door and holding it open for Detective Campbell to exit.

"Here's my card, just in case you want to talk," the detective said, dropping it on the table next to Chubb's bed.

"Fucking pig!" Walid said, closing the door behind him.

The two of them talked for about an hour before Chubb's medication started kicking in. Walid stayed until he drifted off to sleep, and then he went out to get some answers on his own. From what his brother had told him, he didn't know what that shit was about. He wasn't trying to be on that type time again, but when you fuck with family, the streets will mourn. Later that night, Chubb needed to make a call that was important.

* * *

Terrance had his *janaza* at the mosque in West Philly three days later. Being a Muslim, he had to be buried while the flesh was still warm. He was laid to rest at the cemetery in the southwest, right off of Cobbs Creek. Four people got down into the grave as they passed them his body, which was wrapped in a white sheet. They laid him on his side and then climbed out. Everyone took turns with a shovel and placed dirt over the body to fill up the grave.

After they left the cemetery, everyone went back to Terrence's mom's house, where his sisters and aunts made all kinds of food. The house was so crowded that it looked like they were having a block party. It was starting to get dark, so the street lights came on. Everyone gathered around to hold a memorial for Terrance for the last time of the night.

Terrance's sisters were talking to her cousin when her left eye kept jumping. She couldn't shake the feeling that something was about to go down. Her mom told her when she was little that if your left eye jumps, that means bad luck, and she could tell that a storm was brewing. She just didn't know what.

"What's wrong, Cuz?" Nikki asked, sensing the change in her cousin's demeanor.

"I'm not sure yet, but something is about to go down."

"Girl! You are tripping! Come on, they are reminiscing about T."

The girls joined the circle to listen to all the people giving her brother compliments. Nikki stood next to Chubb, who was out of the hospital now, and held his hand. The memorial went well, and after everybody started leaving, Chubb, Nikki, and a couple of other people stayed outside, sitting around, talking, and drinking.

A van was driving through the block and stopped right in front of them. The side door opened, and four men jumped out menacingly with big guns drawn. They were all dressed in black and were ready to kill.

"Move and die!" one man said, waving a machine gun around.

No one moved a muscle.

Nikki was petrified as the men walked up to Chubb and one of them smacked him across the head with the butt of a gun. He almost fell out of the wheelchair, but two of the men caught him. They dragged him over to the van and threw him inside. They all got back in the van and pulled off. Nikki screamed and pulled out her cell phone, trying to take a picture of the license plate. But the van hit the corner before she could. She dialed 911 and told them what had just happened.

They patrolled the whole area, but there was no sign of the van anywhere in West Philly. Nikki was so scared, because her feeling had been right. Now she hoped that Chubb was still alive. Bricks had gone to record some music, so he didn't know what had happened until he came back on the block. There was nothing he could do, so he, along with everybody else, just waited to hear something.

CHAPTER 11

A lot of shit had been going down in the last couple of days. Muthafuckas were dropping off the face of the earth, and nobody knew what had happened. Dev and Nut had been putting in work for their boss, and the streets were now starting to see who was in charge. They were a two-man wrecking crew, but they had a team of niggas that Worlds had put at their disposal, and they were straight killers with nothing to lose. Worlds promised them that if anything happened to them, he would take care of their families.

"Yo, bro! This shit is like taking candy from a baby. We putting in work for big homie, and we don't even have to bust our gun right now," Dev said.

"This shit ain't cool, dawg! I'm trying to put in some work and not sit around here while everybody is having fun," Nut replied while taking a sip of Cîroc.

"We have plenty of time for that," Dev said, taking the bottle from him and taking a sip. "Niggas' teams are weak out here right now, and pretty soon we will own everything."

"Don't you mean that nigga Worlds will own everything? He's the money man right now. We working for him. It's not the other way around."

"For now!"

"What you mean by that? That nigga is very well connected. I'm no sucka, but he can get us touched anywhere!" Nut stated, holding up his .40 caliber. "If you trying to take down his shit too, I'm with you."

Dev knew his boy was a live wire, but he wasn't crazy enough to go at a cartel. They just got out of one beef with the Mexicans, and it would only be them. That was out of the question for now.

"Fuck all that! Let's go hit that last spot. The goons are in the car waiting for us. Load up, nigga!" Dev said.

They both gripped a couple of automatic weapons and headed out the door. They had found out there was a spot on 8th and Shunk where the niggas that shot at them, frequently hung out. It was time to pay them a visit.

When they pulled up to the crib, they could see people going in and out of the house. Dev assumed it was a trap house. He thought about just shooting it up and leaving, but he wanted what was inside.

"Y'all niggas ready?" he asked, cocking back the gun. "We taking everything they got and killing anything moving."

Everybody was locked and loaded, ready to move. Nut was the first one out of the car, followed by Dev and the rest of their soldiers. They were dressed in all black and wore ski masks. The soldiers surrounded the house with the efficiency of a swat team. One of the men knocked on the door, looking like he wanted some drugs. When it opened, Nut stepped out first and fired three shots.

The first shot hit the man who opened the door in the throat, and went straight through the back of his neck. The second and third shots hit him execution style in the head and heart. That's when all hell broke out. The people inside were ready for something like this. They didn't know how the intruders had gotten past the first wave of security, but they sure as hell weren't getting out of there alive.

B.L. was upstairs talking to Major on the phone about the new shipment of heroin being delivered in the morning, when he heard the shots.

"What the fuck!" B.L. yelled, looking at the monitor.

"We're under attack, bro. I gotta go!"

"I'm on my way!" Major said, hanging up and running into the bedroom of his house.

He lifted up his mattress and grabbed his .50 caliber handgun and one of his new toys that he just bought earlier, a Mak-90, that when fired sounded like an AK-47. He rushed out the door to get to his partner. He was only ten minutes away, but he hoped it wasn't ten minutes too late.

B.L. picked up his SKS fully automatic assault rifle and headed toward the action. Two men were walking up the steps in his direction as he let the SK talk. The bullets cut through the men's bodies, knocking them back down the steps. A barrage of bullets started flying his way, forcing him to back off and fall back into his room.

Dev and Nut were shooting it out with four men in the kitchen. Bullets were ripping through the kitchen counter, refrigerator, cabinets, and everything else, but they weren't finding their targets. As soon as one of the men tried to run for the back door, Dev hit him with precision in the head. The man fell through the window, dying instantly.

The other three came up to fire, but Nut had already changed positions and had the drop on them. They couldn't even get a shot off because Nut's MP5 canceled that option, laying down all three men.

Dev and Nut then noticed the work on the table. When they walked over to where the drugs were bagged up, they started stuffing everything into trash bags.

"Find out where they have the money!" Nut yelled to a couple of his men.

Before the guys could make a move, the basement door opened and about five more men came rushing out, taking shots at them. The men who Nut had instructed to find the money were hit over ten times by the assault weapons. Dev and Nut started taking aim practice, knocking the men off one by one.

B.L. was cornered upstairs in his room. He hit the floor just in time to miss the bullets flying through the door. He only had one chance to get out of there alive, and that was the window. As soon as he heard them reloading, he leaped up and jumped through the second-floor window. He hit the ground with a hard thump and rolled. The excruciating pain didn't stop him from getting out of the way of the flying bullets.

Major pulled up on the scene in the middle of the gunfire. He hopped out and let his cannon roar. Men were dropping all over the place. B.L. had made it around the front and was helping Major kill the men who were outside. Inside, Dev and Nut were holding their own, being outflanked by B.L.'s crew but killing all of them.

"The back door!" Nut screamed as he headed for it.

Dev got up and followed him out. When they got to the front of the house, Dev spotted B.L. and Major and fired in their direction.

Major and B.L. took cover behind a car and returned fire. The four men were going at it until cop cars starting appearing from every direction. All four men began firing at

181

the cops, causing some of them to crash or pull back. Major looked in the direction of Dev and Nut. "Another place and time, niggas!" he said.

"No question!" Dev replied as the four men retreated in different directions while trying to elude the police.

Black SUVs came flying down the block in the direction of the cops. Men jumped out with crazy firepower and unloaded on the police officers. The police tried retaliating, but they were no match for the assault team. Cops were dropping like flies as the assault team made sure the men got away, before they jumped back into the cars and pulled off.

When Dev was somewhere safe, he tossed his weapon down a drain and changed out of the all-black outfit he had on. Both he and Nut had put clothes on under the black camouflage, just in case, so they were prepared. Dev made it to the crib of some shortie he was fucking, and knocked on the door. When she answered, he walked in and sat down on

the couch.

"I need to use your phone real quick. It's important!" he

said anxiously.

She didn't even ask questions, because she knew he was

a bad boy. She retrieved her phone from her purse and gave

it to him. He dialed Nut's phone to make sure he was

straight. Nut answered on the fourth ring.

"Who this?"

"It's me, nigga! Are you cool?" Dev asked.

"Yeah. I'm straight, bro. Why you calling from another

phone?"

"Mine's still in the car. I hope they don't find that shit,

or they can link all that shit back to us."

"You should be alright, bro. What the fuck was that, though? Who were those muthafuckas who pulled up and popped off on the pigs?" Nut asked.

"I don't know, but they had some big shit that I never seen before. I'm glad they were helping us," Dev replied.

"I called big homie, and he wants us to meet with him first thing in the morning. People are calling for a truce because everybody is losing money right now, and they don't want to beef no more."

"That's 'cause they met their match. Pick me up in the morning. I'm going to kick it with my shortie tonight," Dev said, looking over at the boy shorts and wifebeater his girl was wearing.

"Okay, be safe and knock that bitch back out, nigga!" Nut said jokingly.

"I got you, nigga!" Dev told him before hanging up.

CHAPTER 12

It had been a couple of days since the big massacre that took place in South Philly. More than ten cops had been killed in the line of duty, and the mayor of Philadelphia and the top brass were livid. They thought it was in retaliation for the shooting that had happened in North Carolina. That was until they saw all the dead bodies sprawled inside and outside the house. The mayor even asked the governor for help, and to declare a state of emergency and call in the national guard, but the governor told him to hold off and let the feds handle it.

The real reason the governor did that was because he was also in the cartel's pocket. He had talked to his employers and let them know there was a snitch in their organization. The mole had given up some valuable information, and the feds were planning to come down hard on them. But because of the cop killings, it was much worse. That was another reason a truce was called. They needed to find the mole and then get rid of him.

Worlds and Fredd were sitting in Worlds's penthouse that he had bought to get away from Chester. He didn't want anybody trying to catch him slipping out there. Dom had been by his side, so he moved her and her daughter in with him. They were making too much money to stay in that place. There would be so many targets on their backs. The stickup boys were always lurking.

"No one can stop us now, bro! The competition is no longer a problem, and everybody knows that we run the city!" Fredd stated, sipping on a glass of E&J.

Worlds sat on the ottoman, puffing on some loud as he thought about all the treacherous things he and his crew had done to take over the city. They had committed so many murders to get that respect.

"Yeah, but where does that leave us now? We lost a lot of good soldiers in the process, and we don't know if it's truly over yet!" Worlds replied.

"Speaking of soldiers, we still haven't heard from Deja yet, and she hasn't answered any of our calls."

"That is strange, but she and that girl are probably out enjoying that money and having some fun," Worlds said, pouring himself another glass of liquor. "I'm hoping the streets haven't taken her too."

"Come on, ock! They knew what they were getting into when they decided to bang with us. It could have easily been one of us lying in the dirt right now. We promised to take care of their families, and that's what's we'll do," Fredd spat, walking back and forth across the balcony. "Besides, since when has the infamous Donte started getting soft?"

"Nigga! I told you about calling me by my government. I'm not getting soft, either. I'm looking at the big picture. Yeah, we are the primary drug suppliers, but I want more. I want to open up some businesses to cover up our illegal endeavors. I do plan on getting out of the game someday, you know!" Worlds explained as the two overlooked the now peaceful city.

"Niggas always saying they are going to leave the game alone, but never do!"

"Well, I'm going to show you better than I can tell you. I'm tired of all the drama and having to watch my back from those alphabet boys or niggas trying to be the man. I have two kids to raise, and they need me around, bro," Worlds said.

"This is our life, man. This is all we know! For as the law or those niggas out here goes, they either get with the program or get deleted," he stated, with a sinister look on his face. "Anyway, what do you have in mind?"

"I was thinking about investing in a couple of things. First, look at what's going on in Atlantic City with the casinos. How about we look into that or maybe some apartment complex?" Worlds asked.

"That sounds good and all, but how the hell are we going to get into that when neither of us has any business experience? We both dropped out of high school and have criminal records. How the hell we going to do that—legally, that is?"

"I can get Dom to get a business license, and we have friends who can help with lenders. You let me worry about that part, and you worry about keeping our money flowing. Speaking of money, let's get out of here and go check on it. We'll let Dev and Nut relax today after all the shit they did. Besides, I have to pick up my kids and take them to Chuck E. Cheese's, since I haven't spent time with them because of the beef."

The two men headed out of the penthouse to take care of their business. As they stepped off the elevator and headed toward the garage where their cars were parked, they never saw the three black SUVs creeping up on them, until it was too late.

The twelve men jumped out, aiming guns at Worlds and Fredd. They wanted to reach for their weapons, but that would have been committing suicide. A man in a black tuxedo stepped out of the middle car smoking a Dutch.

"Gentlemen, my name is Triz. My employer would like to talk to the both of you."

"I'm not going anywhere. Tell him if he or she wants to speak to me, they can meet me on neutral ground," Fredd said, not backing down.

"It's not a request!" Triz said.

Just then, both men felt a sting on the back of their necks. Before they had a chance to see who just had poked them, they fell to the ground. Worlds's eyes started getting heavy, but not before he saw who was holding the needle in her hand. He passed out just as darkness claimed him.

* * *

Oh damn! My head hurts! Worlds thought, trying to focus on where he was.

When his eyes adjusted to the little bit of light coming into the room, he could see he wasn't alone.

Worlds tried to speak, but no words came out of his mouth. That's when he realized his mouth was gagged. He tried to move, but his hands and legs were also tied. He looked for Fredd, and spotted him with his head down. There were at least four other people in the room with him, but he didn't recognize any of them.

Just then, the door opened, the lights came on, and about ten goons wearing masks entered the room. They were followed by two men, one of whom had grabbed him, and a woman. When Worlds saw who the woman was, anger instantly flushed his body.

"I'm glad you're finally awake. Sorry for the inconvenience, but precautions had to be taken for the good of everyone," Miguel said. "We are just waiting for the last person so we can get this party started."

Worlds was trying to say something, but his sounds were muffled by the rag in his mouth. Miguel nodded his head, and Triz walked over to Worlds and removed the gag.

"What the fuck is going on, Miguel? I thought we had an understanding? Why am I here, and what is she here for?" he said, pointing at Neek. "You must want to go to war, so you might as well kill me now."

"Mr. Wilmore, if I wanted to kill you, you would already be dead. I'm a respectable businessman, and I was asked to gather up all of you and hold you, by someone higher than me. However, you will get to know who this lady is very soon."

Worlds's mind started racing as he thought about who would want him and Fredd. He was also wondering who the other three people were, whose heads were covered by pillowcases.

Miguel must have been reading his mind. He signaled over, and one of his men pulled the masks off of each one of the people. It was Deja, Chubb, and someone Worlds never expected to see: Carlos.

If Carlos was a top boss, why the hell was he tied up in a chair? Worlds had many questions that needed to be answered, and from what Miguel had said, the person to answer them was on his way. Was it Evani? Why would he treat his partner like that, and what did he want with him? Why didn't he just call him over to his office? Question after question flooded through Worlds's mind, and there was only one person who could answer them.

"Where is this person?"

"Be patient, my friend. He will be here in a minute, and then all of your questions will be answered. Would you like a drink of water?" Miguel asked his prisoners.

No one responded.

Everyone was scared except for Worlds and Deja. She was wondering why she was there as well. One thing was for sure, if it was her time to go, she wasn't going out like a pussy.

Suddenly, the door opened, which caused everyone to look in that direction.

The man who everyone was waiting for walked in, and they all stood at attention. Miguel met him halfway to greet him.

"*Gracias por venir. Quiero una bebida?* (Thank you for coming. Want a drink?)" Miguel asked, shaking the man's hand.

"*Estoy bien gracias* (I am fine, thank you)," he replied.

Worlds saw who it was, and he couldn't believe who was back in Philly. Chubb also noticed who it was and knew that niggas was in trouble.

The man walked up to everyone who was tied to a chair, and stared at them.

"Why are they tied up?" he asked, looking over at Miguel.

He was about to answer, but thought twice about it when he saw the look on the man's face. "Untie them now!" Miguel barked.

Four goons rushed over to the captives and untied them.

"Follow me. I have prepared a meal. After you eat, we'll talk about why you are all here," the man told them.

Worlds, Fredd, Deja, Chubb, and Carlos all followed the man into the other room, where there was a huge oval table covered with a tablecloth. There were ten plates of food and eleven chairs, but only seven people.

"Everyone sit down and eat," the man said.

They all sat down and started eating.

"I brought you all here because we have a snake in our midst. Somebody here has been giving info to the wrong people, and a couple of my organizations in Florida have been raided, and they're working their way back here. So it's simple. I need to know which one of you has been running your fucking mouth!"

"I hate snitches!" Worlds said, being the first to speak.

He looked dead at the man standing before him.

"We had a long talk before, and I said something to you. Did you listen to anything I said?"

Worlds thought about what they talked about, and was about to respond, until four more people were escorted in at gunpoint. The man didn't even turn around.

"Have a seat and eat up."

It was Dev, Nut, Major, and B.L. They all took a seat and poured some wine in their glasses. The servers brought in meat and placed a piece on each plate.

"This smells good. What kind of meat is it?" B.L. asked as he took a bite.

No one answered. They all started eating while they waited to hear who the snitch was.

Deja already was anxious to know so she could put a bullet through their skull for putting her through this. She also wanted to know who this man was with all the power. He intrigued her.

"As you know, there is one empty seat. That's because he was responsible for hiring all of you, so it's his fault that we have a snitch in our presence," the man said.

"Where is he? I'll kill him for you and everybody else. I'll also body the nigga that's making it hot!" Deja said, standing up.

"That won't be necessary, lil lady. Evani is not the problem anymore. Someone at this table is, though. To answer your question about Evani's whereabouts—" the man paused before continuing "—you're eating him!"

Everybody dropped their forks and started gagging. They couldn't believe what had just happened to them. Worlds hoped like hell that he heard him wrong. When he didn't see any signs of a smile, he knew right then just how crazy this man was.

"Now that I have your attention, back to the matter at hand. Today, someone is going to die for deceiving me and this organization. See, the thing about having power is having everyone on the payroll. I had someone watching all of you, and you didn't even know it. Let me introduce you to the person who has been an agent for the FBI and told me about the mole in my organization. Send her in!" he said to one of the guards.

A couple of minutes later, Neek walked in and stood by the table. Deja was more shocked than anybody because of the relationship she thought she had and all the things they did together, only to find out the whole time she was a fed.

"Don't look so shocked, Deja. You know we will do whatever it takes to get the information we need," Neek told her. "I played on your emotions, and it worked to my advantage."

"I should kill your ass!" Deja stated, jumping up from the table.

Two huge guards immediately aimed their weapons at her.

"Everyone settle down. One of you will be dead by the end of tonight. For those of you who don't know her, I would like to introduce you to Agent Pryor. See, instead of her working with her counterparts, she has been working for me. What better spy than an actual agent. That way I have tabs on both sides. She's the one who gave me the disturbing news."

"So why do you have me sitting here like some fucking snitch?" Worlds asked. "That's not in my bloodline!"

"Because you had that snitch on your team, and it's because of you and your team that I had to destroy a large amount of my warehouses, among other things."

"Fuck am I here for then?" Chubb said.

"Everyone, this is my big brother, right here!" the man said, walking over toward Chubb. "I brought you here to take over the PA organization and to confront the muthafucka that had you touched."

At that moment, two guards grabbed Miguel and relieved him of his weapon. They passed the gun to Chubb, who stood up, holding his stomach; and without saying a word, he emptied the clip into Miguel's body. The guards quickly moved out of the way as his body danced in place. He was dead before he hit the floor. Chubb sat back down ice-grilling Fredd like he wanted to kill him too. He thought it was him that set him up.

The room was so quiet that one could hear a pin drop. Everyone was looking around wondering who would be next. Dev was in deep thought about something, and then it finally hit him. "You're E.J.?"

"That is correct!" E.J. said, looking at Dev. "I know everybody thought I was dead, but here I am in the flesh. It's amazing what money can buy for the right price."

Only a few people were around when he came to the building to see Worlds. That's why there were so many shocked faces. E.J. didn't care who knew his identity now. When he found out that his brother got shot, he knew it was time to appear again, but this time to everyone.

"Now, back to the matter at hand. If there's one thing I hate more than a child molester, it's a snitch. So this is your one and only chance to get right with not only yourself but with God, and confess your transgressions in front of the round table," E.J. said, removing his gun from the small of his back.

He then sat down at the head of the table and waited.

Everyone looked around the table at each other, but no one said anything. They were all suspicious of the next person, wondering who the snitch was.

"You have sixty seconds to admit your guilt. God forgives, but I don't. Deceit is punishable by death in my eyes. I don't care who you are."

That minute seemed like it went by in fifteen seconds. E.J. stood up gripping his gun in his right hand. He walked over to the ninety-inch big screen television hanging on the wall and turned it on. One of his men passed him a flash drive, which he plugged it in.

"I'm about to show you who the person is that was infiltrating my organization. I would have spared you, but you wouldn't confess, and now it's too late," E.J. said, pressing the power button to the television.

When the photo of the snitch appeared on the screen, everyone in the room gasped. It showed a group of people sitting around a desk talking to a shadow. One of E.J.'s men walked over and took the gun that Chubb was holding. He passed it to E.J. and stepped back, because he already knew what was about to happen.

Worlds was shocked and looked over at the screen to make sure he was seeing correctly. The screen wouldn't reveal the face of the person, because it was blurred out. They all remembered having a meeting like that before, so it could be any of them.

"Let's just get this over with so we can get back to business," E.J. announced.

He removed the clip from the gun, replacing it with a fresh one. His men all cocked their weapons and aimed at the table. E.J. started walking around the table, pointing the gun toward the back of each person's head.

"Sorry, but this is just business, and you picked the wrong fucking ones!" he said, stopping and blowing off the back of the snitch's head.

Blood splattered everywhere, getting all over them.

"Now let's get back to work."

E.J. walked out of the room, never looking back at the carnage he had just left.

Coming Soon!

A Hustler's Nightmare

and

Naughty Housewives II: Secrets Revealed

BOOKS BY GOOD2GO AUTHORS

GOOD 2 GO FILMS PRESENTS

**THE HAND I WAS DEALT- FREE WEB SERIES
NOW AVAILABLE ON YOUTUBE!
YOUTUBE.COM/SILKWHITE212**

SEASON TWO NOW AVAILABLE

To order books, please fill out the order form below:

To order films please go to *www.good2gofilms.com*

Name:_____

Address:_____

City: _____ State: _____ Zip Code: _____

Phone:_____

Email:_____

Method of Payment: Check   VISA   MASTERCARD

Credit Card#:_____

Name as it appears on card: _____

Signature: _____

Item Name	Price	Qty	Amount
48 Hours to Die – Silk White	$14.99		
A Hustler's Dream - Ernest Morris	$14.99		
A Hustler's Dream 2 - Ernest Morris	$14.99		
Business Is Business – Silk White	$14.99		
Business Is Business 2 – Silk White	$14.99		
Business Is Business 3 – Silk White	$14.99		
Childhood Sweethearts – Jacob Spears	$14.99		
Childhood Sweethearts 2 – Jacob Spears	$14.99		
Childhood Sweethearts 3 - Jacob Spears	$14.99		
Childhood Sweethearts 4 - Jacob Spears	$14.99		
Flipping Numbers – Ernest Morris	$14.99		
Flipping Numbers 2 – Ernest Morris	$14.99		
He Loves Me, He Loves You Not - Mychea	$14.99		
He Loves Me, He Loves You Not 2 - Mychea	$14.99		
He Loves Me, He Loves You Not 3 - Mychea	$14.99		
He Loves Me, He Loves You Not 4 – Mychea	$14.99		
He Loves Me, He Loves You Not 5 – Mychea	$14.99		
Lord of My Land – Jay Morrison	$14.99		
Lost and Turned Out – Ernest Morris	$14.99		
Married To Da Streets – Silk White	$14.99		
M.E.R.C. - Make Every Rep Count Health and Fitness	$14.99		
My Besties – Asia Hill	$14.99		
My Besties 2 – Asia Hill	$14.99		
My Besties 3 – Asia Hill	$14.99		
My Besties 4 – Asia Hill	$14.99		
My Boyfriend's Wife - Mychea	$14.99		
My Boyfriend's Wife 2 – Mychea	$14.99		
Naughty Housewives – Ernest Morris	$14.99		
Naughty Housewives 2 – Ernest Morris	$14.99		
Naughty Housewives 3 – Ernest Morris	$14.99		
Never Be The Same – Silk White	$14.99		

Stranded – Silk White	$14.99		
Slumped – Jason Brent	$14.99		
Tears of a Hustler - Silk White	$14.99		
Tears of a Hustler 2 - Silk White	$14.99		
Tears of a Hustler 3 - Silk White	$14.99		
Tears of a Hustler 4- Silk White	$14.99		
Tears of a Hustler 5 – Silk White	$14.99		
Tears of a Hustler 6 – Silk White	$14.99		
The Panty Ripper - Reality Way	$14.99		
The Panty Ripper 3 – Reality Way	$14.99		
The Solution – Jay Morrison	$14.99		
The Teflon Queen – Silk White	$14.99		
The Teflon Queen 2 – Silk White	$14.99		
The Teflon Queen 3 – Silk White	$14.99		
The Teflon Queen 4 – Silk White	$14.99		
The Teflon Queen 5 – Silk White	$14.99		
The Teflon Queen 6 - Silk White	$14.99		
The Vacation – Silk White	$14.99		
Tied To A Boss - J.L. Rose	$14.99		
Tied To A Boss 2 - J.L. Rose	$14.99		
Tied To A Boss 3 - J.L. Rose	$14.99		
Time Is Money - Silk White	$14.99		
Two Mask One Heart – Jacob Spears and Trayvon Jackson	$14.99		
Two Mask One Heart 2 – Jacob Spears and Trayvon Jackson	$14.99		
Two Mask One Heart 3 – Jacob Spears and Trayvon Jackson	$14.99		
Young Goonz – Reality Way	$14.99		
Young Legend – J.L. Rose	$14.99		
Subtotal:			
Tax:			
Shipping (Free) U.S. Media Mail:			
Total:			

Make Checks Payable To:
Good2Go Publishing
7311 W Glass Lane,
Laveen, AZ 85339

1|17

CPSIA information can be obtained
at www.ICGtesting.com
Printed in the USA
LVOW13s2219150117
521060LV00007B/678/P